Jonathan Knight
By Darryl B Petitt

Dedication

This book is dedicated to…

All the men and women in our nation who put country first and their own personal safety and comfort last.

Author's Note

As we all know, a fictional story is a story that's not real and non-fiction is a true story. So what is faction? A faction is a story that is a mix of fact and fiction, which is the book you are about to read.

I started *Jonathan Knight* two years ago, and had I not taken time away from it, you would have thought I was nuts for writing a story about the United States becoming Sharia compliant. Today, it's in the headlines and more and more people are talking about the Crusades after our President mentioned it in a speech:

"And lest we get on our high horse and think this is unique to some other place, remember that during the Crusades and the Inquisition, people committed terrible deeds in the name of Christ."

What he failed to say was that the Middle East at one time was predominantly Christian and Jewish. Prior to 600 A.D. there were no Muslims but by 1000 A.D. Muslims had taken over the Middle East and parts of Europe through murderous campaigns.

What our President also failed to say was that if there had not been the Crusades and an Inquisition, most of

Europe wouldn't exist today as we know it. Muslims had taken part of it over and Europeans took it back during the Crusades.

But what happened to the Knights Templar—those who fought to take back their lands from the Muslims in Spain, Italy, and Turkey? In my factional novel, they still exist. They exist to protect Western nations from those who wish to do them harm, including Islamic extremists who feel it is their duty to subjugate us under Sharia Law or kill us. Jonathan Knight and his family are out there protecting us.

May you be inspired and educated by what you read in this book. ~Darryl Petitt

Acknowledgments

Special thanks to…

My many Facebook friends and supporters. Although the majority of us have never met in person, we have shared many very significant events together. We've laughed and cried together as we worry together about the future of our nation.

My best friend, Anna Shellner, our children and the rest of my family for their continued love and support. You guys are my inspiration.

Kylie and Jessica Malchus are both great artists. Kylie did the drawing and Jessica the graphic design for the book's cover. Thank you both. I also prayed to find an exceptional editor that was just as good and I did. Melanie at Elegant Editing did a fantastic job.

To all of you who purchase this book, thank you. I hope you enjoy reading it.

Prologue

The black burka hides my face. I find it difficult to walk in these awkward clothes. Shopping is one of the few things I am allowed to do. I have not changed my religion; it has been changed for me. It has been changed for us all. Our cities, states and federal government have all gone away. The people are still here but life is different now. Our cultures and way of life are different. We are now living under Sharia Law and we are learning to follow these new laws and customs and it isn't an option; it is a must. I have some shopping to do for Steven and me. I know as a woman that I am not allowed to drive without a man in the car or be without an escort while in public. I took a chance on going to the mall anyway. Steve is out of town on business and shopping is part of my life while he is gone. As I arrive downtown there is a crowd gathering along the sidewalk. I am curious as to why people are moving towards the courtyard that is right off the street ahead. I get closer; people come up from behind me. They are in a hurry and start pushing me ahead. I feel like a leaf caught in the swift currents of a river. I try several times to duck into a store, but each time I try to move over to the right, to let those behind me pass, I am prevented from doing so. At least five others have moved beside me while the momentum of those behind me seems to push me forward. I approach the courtyard, and move towards it. No one blocks me from going there. I enter the courtyard and suddenly I realize that I have been shepherded and corralled. Whether accidentally, or purposefully, I am being pushed forward by the crowd. Once there, I find myself near the curb. Ahead of me are two robed men and a third kneeling on the street, praying.

I am not sure what type of ritual this is. I hadn't noticed at first, but one of the two men has a sword. I can hear the muffled anticipation of the crowd. With swift and practiced precision, the man swings his blade and the scene becomes surreal to me. What is this? Is this some type of street magic trick, with a fake head that hits the ground and then rolls and faces the crowd? The blood, squirting from the neck of the man doesn't seem realistic. It isn't until his body hits the ground and starts twitching that it dawns on me that this is not a street magic show. I have just witnessed the minutes before a living and breathing human is executed in the courtyard square in front of what seemed to be hundreds of people—some of them children—in broad daylight on a U.S. street. A man has just been beheaded. There are no screams from the crowd condemning the act. There is only a continued murmur of people talking and discussing the reasons that brought the man to this fate. Then, ahead, I see two men move towards me. I don't like the expressions on their faces. I turn and slip in between several people that are standing next to me. The men are chasing me. My long garments make it difficult to run. I make it to the sidewalk when another man grabs me. He too is a member of the religious police. I scream.

Chapter One

It must have been that scream that woke me up from this nightmare. Visibly shaken, I turn to my husband, Steve. He is lying in bed next to me reading. He asks me if I have been dreaming. I tell him how I had just witnessed a beheading, how the Religious Police had chased me and how I felt that I was about to suffer the same fate had I not awakened. Steve listens to me and then asks me if I have been reading articles or watching videos of Islam on the Internet again. I just nod my head. He doesn't understand why I'd want to put myself through this.

Why do I insist on watching those gory videos of people who did what came naturally to them in lands far away? Steve, like so many Americans, doesn't understand that I, for some reason have taken on not just that issue but abortion, corruption and so many others the world faces. He doesn't understand why I can be so immersed in problems that are so far removed from my comfortable suburban life that he is providing for me, while I am building my website and Facebook following. He tries to calm me down, but he knows that within a matter of days of taking on and absorbing the world's problems and making them so personal, that I will have similar nightmares again. And I will share my dreams in my blog like I had so many others.

~~~~~~

After reading the article about Islam and Jihad, Jonathan leaned back in his chair and thought about what he had just read. Had the author of this article ever been to an Islamic nation in anything except her dreams or through videos she watched? Her story had seemed so real to him. He had been there and witnessed first-hand what she had just described. After all, it wasn't an isolated incident. It happened rather frequently. He chuckled to himself and thought about how hard it would be for someone to believe that undercover spies stopped to read articles on Facebook and in blogs. Julie had become his favorite writer. He followed her on Facebook and when he had time, also read her blogs. He liked her passion. It came through in almost everything she wrote. He could tell that she wanted to make people understand what she had learned about so many things. Besides being able to put her readers into the story, her articles were very factual as well. Some members of the Knight organization had been her followers since late 2007. Discovering bloggers in the late 2000s was akin to finding a good band and then telling all your friends about them so that you would seem to be the one who had discovered them.

His spy family was a group of underground spies from all over the world. Julie didn't know it, but she had become a cult hero and unofficial member of the Family of Knights, an underground group of some of the best undercover agents from around the world. They were also known as black ops, agents whose countries by and large had no inkling that they were also agents for themselves, on their own personal missions to uphold democracy and freedom for the world. As others go to work, come home and go to bed each night, as the world sleeps, the Knight family is out there, keeping them safe or dying trying.

Chapter Two

Julie sat down at her desk and opened her account. As usual, she checked her messages and emails several times a day. There was always too much on which to comment. She wished she could respond to each one of them, but it was impossible. She quickly scanned her emails first. There were invitations to various events, requests for donations to just about everything under the sun, to play Facebook games, just to say hello or keep her informed on various topics. Some of the email senders were people that she chatted with and remembered; others she didn't know. Julie really had no system in place for whose email she read or responded. She scanned them to see if any were urgent. Some caught her eye or jumped out at her. As a strong believer in divine intervention, she often let God be her guide for what she read that day. When she finally finished going through emails and responding to those that she thought pertinent, she moved over to her Facebook group. Later, she opened her blog and responded to comments on articles she'd previously written and finally wrote her article for the day. When she first started, she didn't have a specific number of articles to write. She wrote until she was tired and needed a break. It was important to her to get out as much information as she could. She turned over some things to her featured bloggers. It had become too difficult to balance responding back to her fans and writing. She found that more than one article would result in too many comments requiring her response. While scanning her Facebook messages, she noticed a non-descript message from someone she didn't remember seeing before. There was no particular reason for opening that message, although if someone was tracking the messages that she checked statistically they would find that she nearly always responded to Facebook messages. Facebook was like an old friend to her. That was where her career had started. Facebook was like mental therapy after losing her job and she has some wonderful friends there. She also met some real nut cases as well. The flakes she blocked and deleted. She opened Jonathan's message and began to read. Little did she know that when she opened it, Jonathan's hidden program would open and track her every keystroke from then on. After reading his message she was not sure of what to think. It wasn't the first such cryptic message with someone claiming to be an insider and promising her ground breaking, earth- shattering revelations and information. Some of those ended up on her mental flake list and were eventually blocked from her friends list. This one sounded innocent enough. She thought she'd just wait to see what he had to offer. Julie wasn't a journalist in the sense that she would sell her soul for a big story.

Her goals were to do her part in getting the county back on the right track. She knew that one day she would be a mother, a grandmother and hopefully a great grandmother. She wanted her children and grandchildren to have as good a life and grow up as she had. She just wanted to help make her world a better place. She wasn't doing it for the money or fame even though the money was starting to find her on its own. Her advertisement sales on her blog were growing exponentially without a strong sales force. She, Sarah and Angela were the sales team who mainly performed those duties.

Chapter Three

It was Saturday and Steve wanted to get a few projects around the house done so that he could relax that evening. A nice dinner with Julie and a football game would be just the ticket today. Maybe Julie would stay off the Internet for a night and they could enjoy some time together. He tried not to bother her much during the week. She had finally found something that she enjoyed and it really took off. It had been six months since she was laid off from her job as a Financial Analyst. The economy was horrible and as much as she tried to find another job, she couldn't. So tonight, Steve thought he would cook something. They would have a nice bottle of wine and then enjoy the evening together. *Who knows*, Steve thought, *maybe this would be the night.* They had no children. Julie had been pregnant once, but she had a miscarriage the year before, shortly after being laid off from the job. They already had a name picked out. Earlier in the week, after their doctor's visit, they were lying in bed and talking about the arrival of their baby. Julie turned to face him and said, "Honey, since it's going to be a girl, I'd like to name her Sarah." "Why Sarah?" Steve asked her. "I don't know; she feels like a

Sarah to me. All my life I've thought of names for a baby girl and the other day, it just came to me." Steve found her hand and held it softly. She continued, "I was daydreaming about the two of us. She was about ten and we were at the mall looking at cute little dresses and she said, 'Mom I want this one.' When I saw it, I said, 'No Sarah. You know your dad would never approve of you wearing that.' That's where the name Sarah came from. It just popped into my head and it just sounded right."

Steve looked at her and said, "Sarah it is then sweetheart. Sarah it is."

Steve stopped daydreaming when Julie walked into the room. He quickly gathered himself. He didn't want her asking him what he was thinking about. He didn't want to upset her. She had been through enough in the past year. "What are you doing today?" He asked as she poured herself a cup of coffee. He looked across the room. Julie was wearing a white house robe and slippers. Her hair was beautiful even uncombed. After she poured the coffee, she opened the refrigerator door to find the creamer and said to him, "I have a Skype meeting with a few of the admins from the company; we've got a few things to go over. After that, I'm going to call a few of the reps from our advertisers and go over the ads with them." Julie's web-based group was heavy into politics. Their world had become politics. After losing the job, Julie had immersed herself in politics. She knew her lay-off had been because of lack of business by her company. She didn't blame them for it. She worked there for ten years. She knew her job well. She got along well with her boss and the other workers in the local office downtown. She saw the numbers and she knew they were struggling, just like so many other companies during the recession.

When Gene, her boss, called her into his office; she had a feeling that she would be let go. "Julie..." Gene started. "I want you to know that what I'm about to tell you has nothing to do with you." Julie could only shake her head in agreement. "It's just that we're bleeding money now. We've lost a lot of our clients and the ones we still have are slow in paying. We're not going to make it if we don't downsize. It was a tough decision and one I didn't want to make...but we're going to have to let you go." "Gene," she said, "I totally understand. I know it isn't easy for you." She could feel her eyes start to water. Gene slid his box of tissue closer to her. "Julie, I know it's tough out there, but I've known you for ten years now and I know you and Steve will be okay. I'm hoping that this recession won't last long and things pick up again so that I can bring you back on before someone else snaps you up."

Later that evening, Julie got online and started chatting with her friends on Facebook. She told them about the events of the day, hoping that one of them in town might have a lead for her. There were a few out of town friends that had leads for her, but she knew that out of town wouldn't work. Steve was doing well on his job at AT&T. He had just received a promotion and would not want to move. She didn't really want to either. They had bought their first house together a few years ago and with the real estate market being what it was, it would take six months to a year to sell it and without much equity they would lose too much. Besides, she loved the home. It was located north of San Antonio on the lower outskirts of the Texas Hill-Country. It was a single-story home. They were amazed that the realtor had found such a wonderful place for them. It had everything and more they had asked her to find for them.

The house sat at the end of the cul-de-sac, nestled

in with three others. All were sitting on at least an acre. They had wanted a house with a big yard and this one had that. It also had an amazing view from the back. The road leading to the house was an uphill drive, with beautiful homes tucked away on large lots filled with oak and cedar trees, cactus and other native Texas plants. One had to drive slowly in the neighborhood or risk hitting a deer along the way. They were everywhere. The deer were so accustomed to the people moving into their area that they seemed to have adopted them. Julie remembered the first time they drove up to the property with the Realtor. They pulled into the driveway and when the realtor opened the door, it was everything of which she had ever dreamed. As she entered the front door, the first thing she saw as she looked straight through the high-ceilinged foyer and living room was the view. After she and Steve had walked through the house, inspecting each of the rooms, they both wanted to see the patio. Steve opened the door for Julie and they walked out. The prior owner left the patio furniture for some reason unknown but they were glad they had. It fit perfectly with the patio and the outdoor kitchen and fireplace. The two of them walked over to the rail and looked out. It seemed that from that patio they could see to the end of the universe and they knew they would spend a lot of time out here.

Julie walked over to the breakfast table off the kitchen and she watched the fog lift off the hillside in the distance and the trees in the yard sway gently in the breeze. "So, what about you? What do you have going?" She asked. "Not much, but a lot," he replied. "I have plans to go to Lowes and pick up some stain for the deck. I'll probably get a good start today and if I'm up to it, I'll finish it by tonight. Then I'm going to stop by the grocery store for a few things. I want to cook up something for us tonight. What would you like?" Looking over at him, she remembered why she married him. He was always thoughtful and considerate of her. She knew she had neglected him lately. "Oh, I don't know Steven...surprise me." She said. He asked, "What's new in the world of politics? Didn't you say that someone had sent you something juicy?" With the success of her blog and website, Julie was receiving more and more tips from people.

Some she had chatted with and knew from the Internet. Others, she didn't know. They had befriended her at some point. She didn't know everyone on her friends list. There are too many of them. When she first became active, it started informally. She met some people online and they started discussing their personal problems and they realized how deeply their daily lives had been affected by the people they elected. As their mutual friends got involved in their discussions, their circle grew. It never stopped growing. "It seems juicy, honey…I just don't know the details of it yet. This government never ceases to amaze me. In a negative way," Julie answered. Steve didn't press her. He let it go. Besides, he needed to go. He had a long day ahead and they could always pick it up when they talked over dinner that night. "Babe…I'd better get going. Have fun with your friends online. I'll see you when I get back." With that said, he picked up his keys from the counter and was off. As he pulled out of the driveway he thought about just how far Julie has taken this venture of hers. He knew she was a hard worker, but he had never seen her so committed to anything. This whole online business thing had just started off as a way for Julie to vent her anger and frustration over the economy…but it had grown so fast. She now had more than twenty-five online employees and then there were Sarah and Angela, whom she met at a local Tea Party rally, at which all three of them had been invited to speak. The ladies hit it off instantly. Shortly afterwards, Julie asked them to come to work for her. They became both co-workers and loyal friends. For this Steve was happy. He was happy to see Julie work her way out of depression. Before she met her two friends, she had constantly tried to involve him in the business. He finally explained to her that it might cause conflicts with his job that he couldn't afford to have, but he would support her as much as he could; he just could not get directly involved.

Steve wrapped up his shopping in record time. The hardware store seemed to have more employees working than customers and it seemed both strange and great to have two employees compete to help him find his supplies and give him unneeded advice on how to stain. The grocery store was as busy as usual, but he only picked up a few items—just enough for one meal. A special meal he hoped. He headed for home; traffic was pretty light for a Saturday. Within twenty minutes, he turned into his subdivision. He noticed that the white truck that had been there right outside the gate was gone. He assumed that the two guys standing outside the truck were landscapers; however, the grass hadn't been cut. Maybe they had been called to another job. He punched in the gate code and barely noticed the UPS truck as it drove out of the exit gate. He wondered if he had missed a package. At least Julie was home and would accept it. As he drove through the gate his mind wandered to the first days in the home.

In the early morning hours, while sitting on the patio, he could hear gunfire and booms coming from the nearby military base and faintly echoing in the hills surrounding his house. This was something the realtor hadn't mentioned but it was something he'd grown accustomed to when he came home from his business travels. At first the sounds were annoying, but they had grown on him and it felt comforting knowing that the U.S. Armed Forces were only about fifteen miles away. He remembered that his Homeowner's Association had asked everyone in the neighborhood to turn off porch lights at night to prevent any distractions to the night flights at the post. He and Julie had been forgetting to do that. A year earlier, the wooded area near the base and not far from his home burned. Texas had experienced a major heat-wave. Just walking outside felt like walking into an oven. The local Volunteer Fire Department bravely struggled to stop the fire but was no match for the inferno. The grass-fire quickly spread and then turned into a major burn. Thousands of homes ranging from three hundred thousand dollars to several million were suddenly in the path of the fire as it burned acre after acre. Finally, the volunteers called for help. The closest to help them were the Apache copters from Camp Bullis. The big birds carried large buckets of fire-retardants underneath and dumped them as they flew above the fires. Within several hours, the fire was safely out, avoiding a major disaster.

Steve drove into the driveway and unpacked the car. After that he walked into the house to check on Julie; he figured she'd be on the computer as usual…writing an article or chatting with someone. As an executive for a corporation, he couldn't really afford to choose sides in an election. AT&T donated to both major parties and some third parties as well just in case. "Honey, I'm home," he called, as he walked into her study before noticing that there was no one there. It was odd that she had left this early on a Saturday. Where could she have gone? He noticed that wherever she went, she usually took her purse or cell phone with her. Maybe she was outside walking the property somewhere or playing with the dogs. That had to be it. So he went back out to the car and finished unloading the items for the night's dinner. On his second trip, he noticed that his neighbor to the right was outside working on his lawn. He started to ask him if he had seen Julie but he didn't want to sound like a crackpot if she was just in the backyard or had gone for a walk. If she had gone for a walk, she would have taken her cell phone, he thought. She must be in the backyard somewhere. He continued on into the house and through to the backyard. He looked around. The dogs were laying in the yard sunning themselves. Normally, if Julie was anywhere around they'd be right next to her, but they weren't. "Julie", he called out. There is no answer. "Julie, I'm home." He said a bit louder this time. Still, no answer. Short of a full scale panic, he wondered where she could be. He tried to stain the patio but his thoughts where on Julie and her whereabouts. He put down the brush and went back inside. "Julie, honey. I'm home. Where are you?" Nothing. After checking the house again, he thought it might be time to ask the neighbor if he'd seen her. Luckily, John was still outside mowing. At first John didn't see or hear him walk up. Steve changed the trajectory of his approach so John could see him. When John finally saw him, he turned off the mower. "Hey neighbor, how are you? How's the wife and job?" he asked. "The job's fine, the wife I'm not sure. I went to the store and can't seem to find her. Her stuff's still in the house. Have you seen her this morning?" "No," he said. "When I looked out the window assessing how much work I'd need to do, I saw a UPS truck drive up. She was there then. I saw her answer the door and waved at her, but I don't think she saw me." "Hmm." Steve said. "Okay, I'm cooking dinner for Julie tonight, but we're going to have to get together and barbeque one weekend soon. Hey, when was the last time that you and Beth have gone to a game? I'll see if I can scrounge up a few tickets for the game on the 25th."

Steve had intentionally changed the subject from Julie. He didn't want to worry John about his concern of Julie not being home. Besides, he was probably over-reacting. "That would be great Steve, I'll let Beth know. You know she's a huge basketball fan. She'd really like that I'm sure." Steve walked back across the yard and went inside. He really didn't know what to do next. So he sat down on the sofa and turned on the TV. Should he go out and stain the deck or start dinner? He had an uneasy feeling. After flipping channels, he settled in on a college basketball game and tried to think of nothing else.

The sun was going down over the horizon and started to cast shadows off the trees as Steve surveyed the backyard. There still was no word from Julie and it has been several hours now. If something happened to her, he might be wasting valuable time by doing nothing. Steve did not cook that afternoon. He decided to drive the neighborhood before dark. Slowly, he drove through the neighborhood and didn't see anything. He went inside and called the police. "Hello, Comal County Sheriff's office". "Hi, my name is Steve Carlson and my wife hasn't come home. I left this morning to go to the store and she's been gone all day but her stuff is still here." The dispatcher asked if she could have been at a family member or friend's house. "No, Steve said. "I've called everyone she could be visiting and they haven't heard from her today." "Okay, sir," the dispatcher said. "I'll send an officer out, but nothing can really be done before twenty-four hours." He gave his address and hung up. About twenty minutes after his call, police officers were ringing the doorbell. Steve answered the door. "Hello sir, my name is Officer Jenkins and this is my partner officer Marshall." "Gentlemen, please…come in," Steve beckoned to the officer.

Steve started to explain the events of the day even before they sat down. At the door, Officer Marshall noticed a smirk or slight smile on Steve's face after being introduced. He found it to be odd for someone to have a quirky smile on his face if his wife was missing. He looked around the living room as his partner asked Steve questions and took notes on the event of the day. After slowly scanning the room, Marshall looked at Steve and asked, "Was your wife having an affair or were you guys having any kind of marital problems? "No, not at all," Steve replied. "We are doing great. Nothing out of the ordinary. In fact, nothing at all. We both work and when we have down time, we really get along well. Why do you ask?" "Just trying to get all the details sir." Marshall responded.

Jenkins was done and stood up and extended his hand to Steve. Marshall followed and got up off the sofa.

"Well, I know you said you drove the neighborhood, but we'll drive it again. If your wife contacts you tonight, just give us a call. Here's my business card with my cell number and we'll call it a day. We'll be waiting to hear from you. I'm sure she'll be home soon." Jenkins said out of habit in situations like this. "If she's not home or hasn't called by tomorrow, we'll send out a detective and get to the bottom of it." Marshall added. It had been his experience that couples had arguments over incidents and it worked itself out by the next day. In this case, he had a feeling that there was more to the story that Steve wasn't telling him. After they left, Steve felt no better. Julie was still missing and they were just going to do the same thing he'd already done. Jenkins and Marshall slowly drove through the dark and winding streets of the subdivision. Marshall spoke first. "I don't know; I just get a funny feeling about that guy." "Why's that?" his partner asked. "The house was too perfect. It looked like he had tried to straighten up or something before we got there." "Come on man, the guy's fairly rich. He's probably got a housekeeper. Did you see the size of the house? What are you thinking…that he had something to do with it?" "Yeah, that's what I'm saying. Nothing concrete, just a hunch."

Chapter Four

Julie was startled awake. She was not sure where she was; a few minutes later she still didn't. She just knew that she wasn't home. She knew that Steve would be worried out of his mind. The day had started so normally for them. Steve took off to go to the store to pick up a few things. She was still in her favorite white house robe when he left. She had heard his car leave their driveway. After he left, she sat down at her computer. She logged on to see what her group had been up to from the night before. They were all Patriots and they were all scared. After all, this was still America. Home of the Brave, Land of the free. Wasn't it? What had started out as an extended recession had turned into something more sinister and disturbing, as if the failed economy hadn't been scary enough. She had just checked her email and was starting to look at posts on Facebook. *What was the latest news?* She wondered. She had seen it coming. She saw the explosive growth of people coming on Facebook to air their grievances just as she and her small circle of friends had done. Her network of friends was growing.

The doorbell rang, interrupting her thoughts. It couldn't be Steve; he had just left. She opened the door and saw two guys in UPS uniform. A quick thought flashed through her mind—why two men when there was usually just one? "Are you Ms. Carlson?" One of them asked. After replying in the affirmative she felt the pain. The electricity pierced her mind and played with her thoughts. The pain was excruciating but it did not last long. She must have passed out because she couldn't remember anything from that point on.

Whoever these UPS men really were, they had rendered Julie unconscious. After catching her before she hit the ground, the men quickly carried her outside to the truck. They knew they had little time to waste there. A special compartment had been built in the truck, behind a stack of boxes to keep prying eyes from seeing Julie placed there, unconscious.

The target was now secure in their possession and they headed back to the house to gather up any computer flash drives Julie may have used and to look through her computer. They found several flash drives. One of the men collected them and put them in his pocket as his partner in crime started looking for files, logs and conversations that Julie may have had with a compromised agent. They found nothing there after very skillful searches. The only thing they could see was that Julie was no slouch. It looked like she had wiped the computer clean after each use. The guy on the computer could not help but be amazed at how an average person had cleaned her computer so thoroughly. There also seemed to be some sort of encryption on the system that he'd never seen before. The best he could do since he had been instructed not to take the computer was to leave a tracking cookie on it that couldn't be removed easily and so that he could remotely look at it later and to try to figure it out. "Let's go," his friend yelled, "Time to move; let's get out of here." They had been going through Julie's computer and household for too long now. They had rigged the computer, had neatly gone through most if not all of her possessions and taken lots of pictures. They felt comfortable in knowing that they could research the computer further from their office. Little did they know that Julie's computer would one day track them. As they drove through the exit gate at the subdivision's entrance, they realized how long they had really been there. They saw Steve on the other side, entering the subdivision. He had been gone no more than two hours.

Chapter Five

The phone woke him. Steve had fallen asleep on the sofa watching TV. "Hi Steve, this is Sarah…can I speak to Julie?" Steve cleared his throat. It had been several weeks since he'd seen or talked to Sarah even though she lived only a few blocks away in the same subdivision. "Julie didn't come home last night Sarah. I called you last night and I was going to call you this morning and see if she was at your place or if you'd seen her." After a few seconds of silence, Sarah said, "No Steve, she didn't come by here. I haven't seen her. That's not like Julie. Have you called the police?" Steve said, "Yeah, they came by but they probably thought we'd had an argument and she'd call or something. She hasn't." Sarah told him that she'd be right over. Within minutes she was at the front door. Steve got up and let her in, inviting her to have a seat and a cup of the coffee he had started before falling asleep. Sarah feared the worse. Julie had told her about the strange message and had shared it with her. As soon as Steve told her that Julie was missing, she felt that it was somehow connected with that message. She didn't know how Steve would react to this information. She could tell that Steve wasn't the type of person to believe in things like those in the network did. They spent a great deal of time on the Internet being amateur reporters and uncovered more truths than those who did it for a living.

There were things that went on behind the scenes of government and religions that not too many people believed or cared to hear about in their everyday lives because they only saw things on the surface. However, she needed to tell him. Julie was somewhere and she might be in a lot of trouble wherever she was. So she started. "Steve, you may not want to believe what I'm about to tell you. A few months ago, I wouldn't have believed it either. Someone sent Julie a message on Facebook the other day and unless she's decided to leave you for some strange reason, her disappearance probably has something to do with that." Steve looked at her incredulously and said, "Message, what kind of message Sarah?" Sarah had printed out the message that Julie forwarded to her with instructions to delete after reading. She hadn't. Sarah had folded the printout and put it in her purse before leaving the house. She handed it to Steve, all the while thinking that the reason for Julie's disappearance may have been because she did not destroy the message. She was always careful but this time she may have made a consequential mistake and she felt sick in her stomach. He read the message and then reread it, not fully understanding or believing it. It was silly. It sounded like someone wanted to pretend to be a spy. Was this person somehow stalking his wife? Was this person capable of kidnapping someone or worse? Did Julie agree to meet this person, thinking that the message was real? Steve's head filled with questions like someone filling a balloon with air. That last question was one breath too much and he felt the balloon couldn't take another. "Sarah, should I call the cops again?"

For the first time in years, he was asking someone for advice. On his job, he had worked his way from a mid-management position after college and he knew most of the answers or knew where to go to look for them. This was different. He had never had a loved one stolen from him. He didn't want Sarah to see him cry so he got up and went to the kitchen and pulled a couple of coffee mugs from the cabinet. Sarah rose from the sofa and moved over to the table in the breakfast area. Steve had wiped away the tears and tried to get a hold on his emotions. He had to have a clear head when he made another call to the police. He brought over the coffee, stirrers, sugar and cream. Afterwards, he sat down. His wife was missing and her best friend and worker just told him that some guy had probably kidnapped her. "Sarah, I swear to God, if this guy hurts my wife." His voice trailed off. Sarah spoke, "Steve, it's probably not that guy that has her. It's probably someone in our own government." Steve wasn't prepared for that comment. "Sarah, do you know what you're saying?" He said. "I sure do Steve. There are a lot of things we've discovered over the last few years since the recession started." She continued, "Steve, I hope you don't mind…but I called Christian and Angela and told them Julie is missing. She's in a lot of trouble and I know you're going to have to call the police.

"I just don't think they're going to find her and more than likely, they're going to blame you. Lately, that seems to be the easiest way when somebody comes up missing…the husband is the first person they look at. If you end up in jail, I'd like to have some sort of a plan that involves you, even if you can't be on hand to help us." This was all hitting Steve like a ton of bricks. What is his wife involved in? "In jail?" He asked, "Why would I go to jail?"

Chapter Six

The rain rolled down the small slit that was supposed to be a window at the very top of the back wall. Just beyond the rain-smeared window, Julie could see the grey skies above. Not much else. Dazed and confused, Julie tried to get her bearings but she couldn't. It all had happened too fast. In her mind she was fighting them as hard as she could, but in reality it had happened too quickly. Whatever it was that touched her when those two guys came to her door felt like fire. It blazed through her neck where they had touched her and radiated through her body when she had lost consciousness. Now she was in this place and she didn't know where this place was. This place had been her home for twenty-four hours now. Julie was in a jail cell—something that she had never experienced and had hoped that she wouldn't. Her younger brother had been in jail for just a few nights when he was in college. He had called her instead of their parents to bail him out. He didn't want them to know he had been drinking. She had been thrown in jail without cause. Then she remembered. She had done something. Something that might get her killed. Now she realized the seriousness of her situation. It was slowly starting to come back to her. As she sat on the bottom bunk of the bed that was attached to the wall, she kept going over and over the events that she could remember. Not that it would have done her any good to remember as it looked she wasn't going anywhere and the thought of that weighed heavily on her. Julie was exhausted and laid back on the bed, hoping that by laying down it would calm her down and it did. She laid back and fell asleep. She dreamed she held a baby that was trying to tell her something, but she couldn't understand what. The dream included Steve. Steve walked in and could see the frustration on her face and asked her what was wrong. "She is trying to tell me something and won't stop talking Steve," she said. Steve took the child out of her arms, "Honey, she is just making noise; she can't talk yet. You must be tired. Babies don't talk Julie. She's only a couple of months old, Hon. Look, you go and get some rest and I'll stay up with her." Julie was afraid. "No Steve. You don't understand." She said. "She was warning me that I needed to do something; she needs to finish telling me what it is that I need to do Steve." Steve could tell that she was stressed about something, so he put the baby back in the crib and held her.

Julie was startled awake by the sound of someone walking by her cell. "Why am I here? "She yelled at the door. "Take me home." she screamed. "I didn't do anything. You can't legally hold me like this," she continued. There was no response. She couldn't tell if the person heard or just ignored her screams. From that point on, Julie decided that she needed to control herself if she was going to survive. Someone would be looking for her. Someone would be there soon to make bail for her. It would be all over soon and she could go home and enjoy her house and her husband. It would be great to curl up in bed with a cup of cappuccino on the nightstand next to her bed. A perfect day to catch up on some of the reading she was always behind on. There wouldn't be any reading in bed tonight. There wouldn't be a bed, at least not her king-sized bed, with her husband Steve lying next to her watching TV. The last time she saw him, he was planning a special night for them. He had gone to the grocery store and planned to cook for her that night. Now, her bed was a single metal slab that was attached to the concrete wall. On top of the slab was a thin, stained mattress. There was no comforter—just a somewhat white sheet. There was no night stand—just a sink and a toilet that seemed like it had grown out of the concrete floor. The sight of it could be humorous had her situation not been so serious. *Whoever had designed this cell must have been a man* she thought. He had only looked at functionality and certainly not design. The room had been designed to uncomfortably house two people. However, she was alone in the room. She had been since she arrived. Although the room would have been more suffocating with another person and the idea of using the bathroom out in the open with a cellmate only a few feet away did not appeal to her at all; however it would be better to have someone to talk with, someone who could explain where she was or what time it was and why she was there. She had only been there a little over a day, but it seemed much longer. Julie had never experienced mind-numbing boredom like this before. She had no contact with anyone except the guard-type person who brought her food earlier that morning. Julie couldn't eat it. Her throat was still burning from being tazered the morning before. There was no clock in the room, so she couldn't be sure what time it was. She knew that soon she'd lose concept of time. She'd only have the barely visible light from a small window above to let her know if it was night or day. She had nothing to write with so she would have to try to remember everything as best she could. She was determined to keep one of her eating utensils; they allowed her to eat with metal knife and fork, to her surprise.

Her thoughts turned to Steve and then to her business. *My business* she thought. She was sure her employees would be carrying on. Sarah thought she was silly about making all types of contingency plans for all of their safety when she hired Christian and Angela. Hiring the three of them as the nucleus of her company had been a Godsend. Sarah's age and wisdom made her a great manager for whenever Julie needed her. Sarah was a decent enough blogger and could cover if need be, but she hired Angela as an editor. Julie had seen on Facebook how well she wrote. Angela's writing skills were comparable to, if not better than Julie's, although Julie was a more passionate writer. Those writing skills were very important in the current environment. The current administration hadn't counted on the advent of blogs and Facebook commentary to be the rise of a political underground—an underground that would be the groundswell that propelled Republicans to victory in the 2010 mid-term elections. When Angela told Julie about her husband Christian's interest in working for her, Julie almost told her no. She didn't want to grow the company recklessly but she decided to hire him. Christian convinced her of the importance of setting the company's computers up properly. He had recognized something that she hadn't–the need to keep the government out of their business. He set up modules for key people who she didn't even have on board yet. He was convinced that conservatives needed to start using technology more efficiently to win elections.

He told her that as their organization grew, it would be necessary to have key people in place around the nation and that it might expand into other countries and consist mostly of ex-patriots. Many in the beginning, would be the husbands or wives of soldiers stationed overseas and the wives and young adult children of oil company executives. Julie found them willing to work for free because they believed in her and their country and they wanted to help. She was grateful because there would be no way that she could afford to pay for people of that caliber. Julie really had no idea what Christian was talking about but it sounded good and she gave him the green light to go forward with whatever he thought best. Christian was a wiz at computers. He had been trained by the government which he was now helping to protect her against. He had worked at the Pentagon for most of his career after graduating from West Point with honors. He was now providing Julie's online blog with encryption and modules that would prevent the very same government that had trained him from snooping. There must have been a crack in his system somewhere because she was now in jail. There was no way. These people holding her had nothing on her. Christian hadn't missed anything. They were only suspicious of something. If they knew something she would have been formally charged. They might be trying to incriminate her. She had to stay strong and tell them nothing. She was confident that her capture was part of a fishing expedition. The year before she and her team had decided to plan for such an event.

Planning for something such as one of them being kidnapped sounded far-fetched and remote at the time until she heard some of the war stories about the government's tactics. As a large entity, they had the ability to influence elections and thus protect their corrupt lifestyles. The plan would be that if anyone ended up being kidnapped, then that person would have to convince whoever was holding them that they would be exposed if the captive wasn't allowed to contact the team within three days. Christian had written a company-wide whiteboard that a person being held could either write into directly or submit via email or text. The way Christian explained it to her was a bit crude for someone who was as brilliant as he, but he had served in the military. He told her to imagine a piece of meat floating on a body of water. There would be fish below that would be nervously darting up to grab a bite and then receding back to the depths to prevent being eaten themselves. Above, would be birds who were also feeding. This one piece of meat would be serving two purposes; it would be feeding fish from underneath and birds from above. The whiteboard would do the same thing. There would be a top side that would serve as a feeding source for those who were preening the blog for basic political information or something to add and below the surface there would be her team of people who were feeding off of what looked like nothing from above. The bottom side of the software would be encrypted for protected information to then be disseminated to other key people within the organization and could be done so within a matter of seconds. Others within the organization could be then told on need-to-know basis. If it was something everyone needed to know then that information would be spread throughout the Internet on the surface. Her disappearance would soon be in the news. It would be important for Sarah to get out a story and for now, it might not all be one hundred percent true for her own safety and that of Sarah, Angela, Christian and Steve. At the same time, it would be important for her key people to communicate what the truth was so they could try to find her. The important thing for now was for her not to lose her head. Christian's plan was good but only worked if someone was willing to talk to her or if she had her cell phone; neither was the case. Julie smiled for the first time since her capture. The analogy that Christian had used reminded her of something her dad had always said, "It's time to fish or cut bait". She was either going to remain a victim and 'cut bait' as someone who had lost control of the situation dealt to them, or she was going to fish. Her dad had not raised her to sit on the sidelines and cut bait. It was time to go fishing. She realized that Steve would soon know more about her business than he'd care to know. Sarah, Christian and Angela would be telling him of the danger that she had taken on when accepting that message from that stranger and decided to help. Steve would be furious with her and then he'd cry. They'd be sorry that they made her husband cry; he didn't deserve that from a government that he trusted. None of her crew did.

It was now dark outside as far as she could tell. She dozed off again. She had no idea what time it was when she woke to the guard at her door. He was intentionally making as much racket with the tray cart as he could. "Rise and shine" he yelled as she saw her tray pop through the slot in the door. Julie screamed at him, "Hey, you tell whoever put me in this place that they're going to be sorry. If my friends and husband haven't heard from me within three days…all bets are off. Whatever you think I have, if I have it the whole world's going to have it by 5:00 pm on my third day gone." *What had she just done?* She thought. She must have been really asking to be killed. They nearly killed her bringing her here. Julie stood up and walked the six feet to her cell door. She picked up the tray and sat back down with the tray in her lap. Her body was screaming for a cup of coffee and sugar, mostly sugar. It's amazing how quickly the human body craves sugar after not having it. Had the guard said anything else? He didn't say a word as usual. *Where do they get these guys?* She wondered. The least he could have done was tell her to shut up. It was three in the morning, but Julie didn't know that. The government used various methods of mind control and serving meals at odd times to help bring about mental instability was one of them. Her last two meals had been sandwiches.

Chapter Seven

The doorbell brought Steve back to reality. It was Christian and Angela. They rushed over as soon as Sarah told them about Julie's disappearance. "I am sure the government took her Steve," Christian opened the conversation. "They are not too happy with some of the discoveries we made and think we have more information." Steve thought for a moment about what Christian had just told him. Julie had mentioned to him that Christian retired from a distinguished career at the Pentagon when she told him about hiring Angela and Christian to help build up her blog, Facebook page and website. Did she even know what they had built and what a dangerous game they were undertaking? He leaned forward and asked Christian, "Where is my wife?" When the five of them had gone to CPAC together, why had no one told him of the dangers? "Steve, I don't know. I promise you we'll do everything we can to find her though. There is no way we won't. We had no idea that our government would do something like this. Steve, I worked for the government and nowhere in our Constitution does it say that the government can legally kidnap an American citizen but lately our Constitution does not mean much. A law was recently passed allowing them to hold a person indefinitely if accused of terrorism. What we are doing is far from anything like that." "Then what the hell are you guys doing, Christian? I mean come on. I go to the store for a couple of hours, I come back and my wife is gone. What am I supposed to think? What am I supposed to do?" Sarah thought it time to step in. "Steve," she said, "This message…we just got a few days ago and weren't really sure we were going to do anything with it.

I forwarded it to Christian and Angela when I got it. I thought we'd let Christian take a look and see if the guy sending it was just some crackpot. He's not. As Christian told you, he set up a form of communication for us so that nobody not even the government would be able to see what we were discussing." Steve asked Sarah, "Why would you even need to talk in such privacy? What were you guys thinking and why are you playing around like that? Where is this going?" Angela spoke for the first time, "Steve, we're Americans. You have to see what's been going on here. You work for one of the oldest and largest companies in this country. You can't tell us that you haven't noticed what's going on. You may not have wanted to do anything about it for whatever reason, but we do and we are. Julie wanted to and she is. None of us wanted this to happen and in fact we are fighting because we knew it could happen. Look Steve, Julie didn't want you involved. You guys have been together since college. She's seen how hard you've worked to get to the job you have and she knew that you couldn't afford to get involved. She is aware that the more you knew the more you'd want to protect her. Steve, she wants to protect you. She is trying to protect your job." Angela was no wallflower. She told Steve what they were all thinking…but they knew he was hurting and didn't want to add to it.

Angela slapped him with her words and snapped him out of his anger. "Look. I'm sorry." Steve said. "I just don't know what's going on and I want my wife back." Steve put his hands to his face to hide his tears. Sarah stood up and stood next to him to console him, gently rubbing his back. Christian reached over to the napkins on the table and handed one to Steve. Sarah wanted to show Steve the other message they had received. She felt they owed him that much but she had not brought it with her.

She knew Christian and Angela had received some that she didn't have. She asked them. Christian stood up and pulled the flash drive from his pocket and without saying anything placed it on the table. Sarah spoke, "Steve, like it or not you're going to have to be a part of this now. We have to include you in everything. You're going to need to call the police back as soon as we leave or we'll stay with you while you do, if you like, but they can't know anything about what we're about to share with you because getting them involved may endanger Julie's life. You're going to just have to play this through and not say anything. Christian, Angela, I didn't bring my flash drive. I just hurried and came here. I printed out the first message, but I'll need to run home real fast and get it. Can you stay with Steve until I get back? I'll be gone only a few minutes."

With that said she left. Each had a sense that this was not the time to take chances. Julie had already been kidnapped and they didn't even think to have at least one of them go with her. Christian said to Steve, "Steve, we'll be right back. We're going to Sarah's. We aren't thinking straight. We shouldn't have let her go alone. We'll be right back. Angela, let's go." The drive to Sarah's was only a few minutes away.

As they drove up they saw the UPS truck and the two drivers leaving the front door and rushing to the truck. The truck sped out of the driveway and down the street before they could park. Christian and Angela thought nothing of it at first. They were used to the fast pace and tight schedule that the company kept. It seemed that Sarah had good timing to leave Steve's when she did or she would have missed the package, whatever that was.

They thought that until they got to the front door and saw that it was still slightly open. Christian called out, "Sarah." He didn't finish his sentence and almost tripped over Sarah who was lying unconscious a few feet from the entrance. She was breathing. Angela screamed and Christian immediately pulled out his cell phone and dialed 911. "911 emergency." the voice on the other end said. "Hello, our friend's been hurt. Two guys just left. They were driving a UPS truck. They were running off when we drove up. We need help. Angela, what's the address here?"

He handed Angela the phone and started doing CPR on Sarah to aid her breathing. That's when he noticed the burn marks on her neck. "Angela, tell them she's been tazered." While waiting on the EMS they called Steve who was there almost before they hung up with him. In the meantime, Sarah came to. She saw the three of them around her and recognized that she was in the foyer of her own home. Anything else she couldn't remember. Christian relayed what they had encountered while driving up. Sarah had a foggy memory of what happened.

It was all so fast. She had gone into her study to get the flash drive. She knew exactly where it was. It was in her desk drawer. She felt in her jean pocket where she had put it and it was still there. The drivers didn't have time to get it. Christian and Angela's driving up must have scared them away. After hearing this, Steve remembered what he had been told by his neighbor.

He remembered that the neighbor said that he saw a UPS truck in his driveway before Julie disappeared. He then remembered seeing a UPS truck exiting the subdivision gate as he was coming from the store that Saturday morning. They now were starting to see a clearer picture and fortunately, Sarah was okay.

Chapter Eight

Steve was sitting on the patio thinking about Julie and where she might be and his mind wandered to the events of the past year. What a thrill CPAC had been. They were there with the heavy-weights of the party and she was there with her favorite people, her husband and her three new best friends Sarah, Angela and Angela's husband Christian. They arrived on Thursday night. On Friday morning, a whole day of exhibits and lectures had been planned. He decided to take in several speeches with Julie and her group, then go back to the hotel room and watch television. In that way, he would be giving Julie a chance to really enjoy the experience with her friends who were more in to the whole political thing than he was. Plus, it gave him a chance to just enjoy some time off, relax and watch a few games. He ordered something from room-service and just vegged out for the rest of the afternoon until Julie got back. From there, they got dressed in their best formal wear and attended several of the balls and mixers.

He was in for a very long weekend, but if it made Julie happy he was all for it. Friday had gone according to plan. After several conferences on party politics, walking through rows and rows of campaign paraphernalia and other political items ranging from t-shirts to toilet paper embossed with the image of a liberal candidate, Steve had decided it was time to retire to the hotel room. Christian, Angela, Sarah and Julie kept walking through the auditorium meeting and greeting fans, signing autographs and letting members and future members of their group get their fill of taking pictures. It seemed that everyone had recently written a book. Julie hadn't slowed down enough to write one. The only one in their group who was working on one was Christian and Julie had promised him that as soon as he was done she would help him promote it on the blog, website and at events. She wasn't sure where Christian found all of his time. He was surely an amazing man with a lot of accomplishments and hobbies. He was nearing completion of his first book titled "The Christian Church and Their Role in Counter-Terrorism." Julie wasn't quite sure how he could make a complete book on the subject.

It seemed as if the modern church had no role in terrorism and although she knew of the struggle between Muslims and Christians and how it had gone on for centuries, it appeared that the church was no longer involved, having instead turned that role over to the governments. She wanted to ask Christian about the connection but she didn't for two reasons. First, people writing books are often as secretive about the subject matter as engineers and scientists are who are working on a patent for a new discovery. Second, she knew that because of his involvement with counter-terrorism and his previous job at the Pentagon, she did not want to put him on the spot. Anyway, Julie never did ask the question.

Julie's speech at CPAC was quite an honor and Steve was proud of her. Unfortunately, he didn't understand all the fuss. He met the Presidential candidates during his business travels. Celebrities and others of that ilk needed to be entertained to keep AT&T in the forefront of the minds of movers and shakers. Sometimes he would go, sometimes one of the other Vice-Presidents would go or on other occasions several of them went together. There was NASCAR, the Kentucky Derby, football and basketball games to attend among others. Julie did not blame him for wanting to go back to the hotel room and watch one of the events in comfort. Even at events that were not sponsored by AT&T, the company usually had either premier or box seats. These tickets were used to promote the company. Some lucky company owner or friend of a friend would be given a pair of tickets to attend the event. Steve would be there as a company representative and he met a lot of good people but also some that he wanted to strangle after just a few minutes. Lucky for them he never did. On more than one of those occasions, it had been a politician. Over the years, he saw the who's who as well as the who wanted to be a who's who and he had developed quite an instinct for sorting them out and putting them in the right category.

So to Steve, CPAC was just another event, allowing people who may never see each other again in life to tell each other that they'd have to set an appointment for lunch. They very seldom did. After a drink or snack somewhere, he'd head back to the hotel room and then call Julie to let her know he was fine and to check on her. He was pretty sure he knew half the people at CPAC and had their personal cell numbers in his contact list. For Julie, this was her first big event and for that he was excited for her.

Chapter Nine

Today's struggle among Islam and other religions began before Christ's birth. It began with Ishmael, son of Abraham, the father of the Arab nation. When Jonathan lived in the Middle East during one of his missions with the CIA, he heard Arabs speak about the Crusades as if the Crusades happened yesterday. The formation of the Knights Templar was estimated from between 1129 AD and 1312 AD—the time period when the Knights Templar defended Christianity against Arab marauders. The year 1312 AD is when rumors started of the Knights being either killed off or disbanded, but they hadn't been disbanded. The group no longer represented the Catholic Church. Their goals had been expanded and became bigger than any one church or nation. The purpose had grown to include Christianity primarily but also the religious freedom for others around the world. They fought for religious freedom and democracy.

The "Muslim" struggle against Christians has gone on for centuries and Muslims are very passionate about it. People who are from Western nations, for the most part, have forgotten all about the Crusades. They may only think of Abraham, Ishmael and Hagar in Bible study or hear it in a sermon but just as quickly put it aside and out of their minds as they go on their daily lives. It became quite apparent to Jonathan that Arabs do not. Most Arabs lived it in their daily lives and daily prayers.

Religion is their daily life. By being required to pray five times a day, Muslims have no choice but to think about religion. It has been that way for centuries and will more than likely continue to be. There's no comparison to how much more seriously Muslims take their religion compared to the lukewarm westernized Christians anywhere in the world. To Jonathan, the Muslim "problem" in Western nations became painfully clear. It was one of the most serious problems facing his country.

Muslims had vowed time and time again to subjugate citizens of other religions but first give them an opportunity to convert to Islam before killing them. Many Westerners would blow off this kind of talk and not take it seriously. However, Jonathan and cohorts in the Knight organization knew the truth. The struggle was very real for all of them and was a daily matter of survival as they tried not to slip and give away their real identities. Of course Muslims want everyone to believe they have no ill will towards Westerners, until they catch some poor unsuspecting missionary or Christian traveler in a vulnerable position and cut their head off like it wasn't supposed to be there.

It is the stated goal of Muslim governments to overwhelm the United States from within, without needing to fire a single shot and therefore ideologically rule the world. Jonathan wasn't a political man, but he realized that it was the unspoken goal of the U.S. politicians from both parties to take money from Muslims and look the other way when they moved their agenda forward. And Muslims aren't alone in trying slice up the country and bring it to its knees economically, socially and spiritually. Communist nations like Russia and China were different. Their goal it is to infiltrate and run for office in nations that they consider financial adversaries. Elected officials throughout the west helped Communist and Muslim governments by running interference on Americans' who are not paying attention to what is going on and who are not asking enough question. By keeping their citizens fearful; they could control them and take away their rights and liberties. Jonathan had heard the rumors that 9/11 was an inside job. There are a bunch of conspiracy theorists that embraced the idea that the CIA or Black Ops were responsible for the events that happened that day. If it was a CIA or a Black Ops operation, Jonathan had heard nothing of it. Some things would never be known. As a CIA agent, then Black Op and now Knight; he himself had been involved in operations that would never be known by anyone except the people that were dead and those who killed them. They helped carry out the missions and none of the dead once were going to talk. Jonathan noticed that many Muslim's were hell bent on destroying Israel, Europe and the United States, although Russia and China are not off the table. They just aren't as easily accessible. On almost every mission; Jonathan and those helping him, were outnumbered when they hit their targets They would either hike a mile or two to the encampment that they needed to infiltrate, or be dropped in by helicopter. It would depend on whether or not stealth or speed was needed. The choppers made a lot of noise. The enemy would hear it and know to prepare. They wouldn't have more than a few minutes to prepare but that would be all it took for them to get off a few lucky rounds and put Jonathan and his troops at risk. Either way, they'd need to be out by sun up and hopefully back to the base for breakfast. At times, the march, if they decided to do that, would be straight up the side of a mountain to get a better look at the enemy. That was one of Jonathan's least favorite types of missions. The climb was at night using Night Vision Goggles. They would be tired by the time they found a spot to start an assault. After catching their breaths and getting a look at the enemy camp from the higher vantage point, the fighting would begin. When it was over, the captured women and children had to be contained to a given area and then the women would be questioned by an interpreter. All other Ops were taking photographs and rummaging through drawers and desks looking for intelligence. The radio operator would by then have called for transportation before other enemy forces in the area could mount a counter strike. The helicopter landed. There are tense moments before they are at a high enough altitude to speed out of danger from RPG's and small arms fire. Jonathan's new job with the Knight's didn't take him far from his training and experience, he still was doing almost the same thing except he wasn't wearing a uniform and the forces they'd have to battle weren't guerrilla fighters as much as; they were guards that were guarding heads of States, Dictators and Autocrats. It was missions along these lines that brought men and women from various nations together. Little by little each of them had grown tired of risking and wasting their lives to defend countries not sincere about being defended because of money involved. Each mission could be the last for any of them however within twenty-four hours someone would replace them. It became more important to Jonathan, as he grew older, that the risks he took should not be in vain.

Chapter Ten

Jonathan Knight wasn't his real name. In his career with the Central Intelligence Agency, Jonathan had assumed many names and the government made each of them appear and disappear at will. He would get a call from his commander and be instructed about the assignment and new identity. Shortly afterwards, he'd receive a file with the vital statistics of the person that he would become. Sometimes it would be a living being that more than likely was no longer breathing for some reason or other. Usually, if the person had been alive at one time, the Agency would try to match an agent with the person's physical characteristics. In Jonathan's case the person would need to resemble as closely as possible a black or Middle-Eastern male from any country in the world. Part of his assignment was to then study the country, the region, traditions, language and town, down to the street of the person.

Then, he would need to master the accents and mannerisms of that person. That often required a visit to the area for several days to weeks. He was allowed to stay only for a limited time in any given area. People wander in and out of places all over the world, often attracting little attention unless they stay in one place for too long. "In real life", was a term that Jonathan had no understanding of after a few years on the job. He was often gone from the place he once called home. Now, he could call a lot of places home. There were several women from his time with the Agency who still could claim to be his wife, none of whom he had contact with any longer. He left his disappearances from those women's lives up to the Agency to clean up after he was gone. In some cases it would also mean making his wife and other members of her family disappear as well.

At least he had gotten none of them pregnant he thought, at least that's the story he told himself in order to stay sane. His travels had taken him all over the world; he had been to Jamaica several times. He had been in Europe and too many other places to remember. His favorite assignments and most difficult were usually the Middle East. These people were such a tight-knit group. Many never left their village to move about to other areas unless it was for religious travel and even then, they would travel with longtime friends. He had found that religious travel or pilgrimage was the American Express of the Middle East, but one's story must be extremely tight when there. One name dropped and the person it was being dropped on could easily verify it. If your story didn't match, it could easily get you killed. He had grown accustomed to the thought of possibly losing his head on a mission. When you lost a head in the Middle East it was quite literal and there was no need for interpretation. There would be no discussion and no explanation needed on their part. If someone knew of some law or custom that you broke, justice could either be as quick as a few hours or as slow as few days. They might decide to toy with the person, like a cat delaying the inevitable for a mouse, to make the event more lasting and enjoyable to everyone except the poor soul who was about to be executed. That person would more than likely be tortured in some type of local ritual to Allah before his neck met the razor sharp edge of a blade or course roughness of a homemade or more expensive imported rope. The executioners were usually men of importance in that community and take their job very seriously. Their blades are always as sharp as possible so the victim doesn't suffer. Other communities had no formal position on executioners, so they would take the next best leader and thrust him in that role, whether he had the opportunity to take a life before or not. After losing virginity for Allah, the community celebrated in various ways. The celebrations usually started before the poor guy laying on the ground stopped twitching.

That was in the beginning. Now, Jonathan had traveled there so many times to different regions that he knew what he could and couldn't get away with pretty easily and changing his regional mannerisms and accent came second nature to him. Over time, he started to realize just how many other agents were in the region—agents from all over the world. At times, they watched each other. Over time, he got to know them and develop fragile friendships because most could not be trusted. Those gradual friendships, where each knew the other was an agent for some country but never said so and never wrote anything on paper, slowly developed over the years. They had a very uneasy friendship but usually one in which one would give his life for the other because most of them were on the same side and there for the same purpose of helping their country.

Out of these networks of spies a community of spies started to develop, an international super-agency that operated independently of any government. Long before Jonathan had joined this "family" it had become the Knight family, named after the medieval knights who went on Crusades to protect Christianity from Muslim marauders. Cole Anderson had been in long enough to become one of the elders in the family. How long? No one was really sure. It was best that way. If any of them were ever captured, it would be hard to make someone talk about something they didn't know. The Knight family tree had independent branches. Somewhere out there, there were other branches reporting to the tree. Jonathan knew he could find them if he needed to, but so far he hadn't. His branch was often more than enough to handle. He knew that if his was anything like the others, they had just one assignment at a time and it was up to them to determine the best way to carry it out. Their mission was to protect and defend Christianity where it was found or if it couldn't be found there to get it started.

Money would never be an issue and the lack of it would never be a stumbling block for any of them. The governments that sent them on assignments were not aware of the existence of the Knight family. Most never knew who these undercover agents were. At times they were told an agent had been killed in the line of duty, only to be replaced by another unknown face. They did not realize that some of their agents only remain employed by that government to gather information from the inside or other information from within that country. All agents were aware that at any given time, their own government could turn on them and either fire them or worse, kill them. Each government had a way of eliminating an asset that had become a liability. There was animosity and distrust to a great degree by the agents toward their own government. This sometimes stifled their mission; however their love of country kept them going. Similar to the United States or any other government, whenever there was a change in leadership, the new leader could change their mission. On the other hand, because of a lack of trust in anyone they didn't know, the leader could also have them extinguished. It was usually during these times that the Knight family grew. Agents unable to trust these new leaders would look for protection, and they found it within the Knight family.

This shadowy group often tested new members by giving them assignments that would test both their loyalty to their new family and their bravery. Within a few years of joining, Jonathan had become a leader in his branch. He and Englishman Peter Knight had not met in the Middle East. They had worked several assignments together in Europe and they bumped into each other in Jordan. Each had given their respective governments information on the whereabouts of Osama Bin Laden. Neither government acted on the information after having put both of these agent's lives at risk. At that point, knowing the intentions of many in the Middle East, they decided then and there that it would become their life's work to end this march of the Muslims to rule the world under Sharia Law. They started creating identities under the services of the Knight family. Killing off their identities had been easy. Both the United States and English government had been cavalier towards them. Agents were merely expendable pawns, treated no better than any field grunt in any branch of the military.

The information they risked their lives to gather was systematically filed away, only to be used if a politician ever needed to cover his ass or make headlines. Leaving an agency that was disorganized and treated its agents with little regard was easy. The appointed Director of that Agency was more afraid of a news camera and reporter reporting a bad story on him than he was of any foreign nation plotting against his nation. This ignorance combined with arrogance could easily get the men needlessly killed and for what? They would just end up being another report that would be filed and then forgotten.

Peter and Jonathan quietly joined the Knight family. The family would serve the best interest of truly advancing the goals of the citizens of Western nations and of Christianity. The family was funded by several unknown wealthy western organizations and individual benefactors with complicated bank accounts and a penchant for looking out for their own interests. No one really knew how much money was in the Knight account for them to use, but they knew it was there when they asked for it. A wealthy Western benefactor would not know where the money was going or who was on the receiving end. They had only been told by the closest of their friends to donate money for the benefit of Western causes and then not to ask any questions. Many gave and had for years. On the other end of the spectrum, Muslims, Communists and others had their own streams of money being funneled similarly into such accounts, where wealthy benefactors from around the world deposited money that would eventually end up in accounts that would then be used by those dedicated to furthering the causes of Sunni, Shi'ite, Communist causes, etc. For Muslims, that cause was Mohammed and Sharia Law.

For Christians in Western nations the cause was Christianity and freedom. It had been this same cause that had divided the world since shortly after the death of Christ. The Knights Templar had fought the same battle with Muslims centuries before and now it was Jonathan and Peter, new members, who revived the battle for Christians of Western nations to get a foothold into the close knit tribes of the Middle East. Just like their namesakes, members of the Knight family sometimes had to kill to move forward in the protection of Christianity. It was their mission to spread God's word by going into hostile nations to do so. Many in Western nations had become too soft to do that. Being soft was going to get them enslaved as a society by those who were willing to kill or be killed for the love of their religion and its leaders. Not if Jonathan and Peter had anything to do with it. Funding was not a problem…finding people of true faith and conviction was. A wrong move on their part could mean death to either of their physical beings and to freedom and Christianity as far as they were concerned.

Why God had chosen Jonathan and Peter to play a role in this new reformation no longer was a question that would keep either of them up at night. They were Knights and there were others; they just had to find them. They found many willing to drop everything and follow them, just as they had done. God had called them to be both mercenaries and missionaries to bring people back to salvation or do their part in sending them to hell. Too many Communists, Muslims and other godless people denied Christians their freedom to worship for far too long, in lands where they persecuted, tortured and murdered Christians. For too long, they refused to accept that theirs was God's land too. Western leaders and the official churches not only allowed this to happen, but were encouraging it. For money, they were selling their souls to the devil and often discouraged Christians from practicing their faith or duties as called for by God. Something was wrong.

The mission as prescribed by God for them was not just love; it was to bring his children back to the Kingdom of God and there were those willing to die for that.

Many Christians have been tortured or killed for their faith in Christ in the past and it is still happening far too often today. Greedy and corrupt Western leaders allow these atrocities to happen by "turning the other cheek" as they fill their pockets with blood money and their souls with death.

Chapter Eleven

Jonathan wasn't a genius. He did decently in high-school and got by in college as far as he was concerned. A casual observer would disagree with him considering his grades and his accomplishments in class and on the basketball court. His father had served as a mechanic in the Air Force and his mother was from Germany. They met while his father was stationed at Rhein-Main Air Force Base in Frankfurt.

At 6'4 and with natural athletic abilities, he excelled in sports and with a German mother who wanted her children to not just focus on sports, having good grades was mandatory. "Jonathan, look at your hair," his father said to him one day when got home from basketball practice in his last year of high school. "What's wrong with it?" he asked. "It's too long; you'll never get accepted into a decent college with those dreadlocks." Jonathan's dad said. His dad was wrong. He finished high school in the top five percent and being half black during a time when affirmative action was being pushed in the States, he had several Ivy League Schools wanting to give him scholarships for both academics and sports. He settled on Stanford.

When he got there he was surprised to find out how much his parents had rubbed off on him. He didn't do drugs or talk against the government and although he was popular because of being one of the star players on the team, he never felt like he belonged there. Instead of transferring, losing credits and spending extra years in college, he quit the basketball team and picked up another major. Jonathan found his studies in the still developing field of computer programming to be interesting. He decided to hedge his bet on getting a job with another major and decided on International Studies.

It was those courses and discussions about what was going on in other countries that caught his attention. One of his favorite professors was an Arab woman whose family had left Saudi Arabia and had never looked back. Since they weren't part of the Saudi Royal family, her parents had had enough of being treated as second-class citizens. On a vacation to visit relatives in Stockton, California, her father decided that he wasn't going back. He wasn't going to raise his children in such a restrictive life after seeing the joy on their faces when he took them to see their first movie but it was the Children's Museum that got him. He wasn't taking his family back in time to a life of extreme control.

In the museum, he could see that toddlers and children were being exposed to more life experiences than most adults in Saudi Arabia. It wasn't that Saudi Arabia didn't have good schools, she told Jonathan one day after class; it was the fact that there was more to learn about life than religion. Her father realized that learning was living and if a person is not living then they're surely not learning. He applied for asylum for himself and his family. It wasn't easy for him but eventually he became a citizen and with hard work his dream for a less repressive life for his family was realized. He never looked back and he never saw the family members he had left behind again.

Jonathan liked this professor. He admired her openness with him; he wasn't just another of her hundreds of students. She took the time to occasionally meet him for coffee after class and discuss her opinions on the world at large and particularly how Middle Eastern and Western nations were like a scorpion and spider trying to determine which would win and not be eaten. Her assessment was that the United States was being eaten from within, making the job easier for its enemies. The nation was an open society and people from all over the world were there, and some didn't have the best of intentions for living in the United States. It was a lot easier to destroy an open society than a closed one, she told her young student. She told him of many students that came through her classes that were honest with her because she was Arab. They told her of their true intentions for being in the United States. Some were sent by their government, others by their religious

Mullahs, who were Islamic Fundamentalists that wanted to subjugate anyone that was not a Muslim. They all needed technical education that they could not get in their own countries but the intended use of this education was not always for the good.

As Jonathan got closer to graduating, his studies kept him away from his discussions with his favorite professor but she had made an impression on him that would last a lifetime. One day after class, Jonathan went to the student center to mail a letter to his parents to let them know he was doing fine. His parents had decided to retire in the States and had bought a country home in Texas. Jonathan shouldn't have been surprised by their decision; however he knew that it was not an easy decision for his mother to leave her aging mother behind. However, her brothers and sisters were still in Germany and would be there to care for her.

As he walked through the Student Life Center at Stanford, he saw the tables lined along the walls and students milling about talking to representatives of companies about jobs. He slowed his pace and started reading the names on the signs taped to the representatives' tables. He had almost forgotten that this was the reason and end result of his education at Stanford. He had been learning a great deal but didn't seriously consider until now what he would do with the education. He was not surprised that there were no students milling about asking questions at the military recruitment tables which included the FBI, CIA and other agencies. Most Stanford students, as liberals, would not look at a career of service, unless it was as a politician or work for a non-profit.

Something drew him to the CIA's table; the guy sitting behind the table looked to be only a few years older than him. Jonathan feigned a sort of disinterest, thinking his chances of landing a job with the CIA were remote. The representative spoke and asked him, "Are you interested in a job with the CIA?" Jonathan thought to himself for a second and responded to the question while scanning through some of the literature about the CIA that was neatly stacked on the man's table. "I don't know. I'm really not sure what I want to do yet." Jonathan commented. The guy asked him if he'd be interested in an interview. "Sure, why not?" Jonathan said, still trying to sound neutral. Jonathan filled out the questionnaire he was given and went on his way. He had never thought of a career in the CIA and didn't think too much of it as he went to mail his letter on his way back to his room to study.

Graduation had come and gone too soon. His parents were able to attend the ceremony; they flew in from Texas earlier that morning. His father asked him about job prospects and if he had any. Jonathan told him about the interviews he'd gone on with the CIA and told them he had accepted the job. His father was proud of him but his mother was concerned. "Don't worry ma." Jonathan assured her. "It's not that bad. It'll be a piece of cake. I come from good, smart stock and do you really think I'd put my neck on the line if I didn't have to?" His mother wasn't stupid. She knew he was only trying to put her mind at ease. However, she knew she had to let him go and live his life. She knew all that she could do was pray for him and let him go.

The training was extensive. He, as usual, excelled and reveled in the challenges of each test of endurance. He was still young. Even though he had quit the school's team he had worked out in the gym regularly and was always looking for a game of pickup basketball around campus. He had done some training with members of the SIS in counter-terrorism and surveillance and was starting to understand the inner-workings of espionage. To understand the criminal mind, he received the best training money could buy. He was learning that devious and unacceptable behavior was relative, depending on whether or not it had been sanctioned as legal by the government or law enforcement agency of that particular country or region. Things that were deemed illegal in the United States were legal in other places and the U.S. took advantage of that when it was needed.

He found that in most countries in the Middle East, it was almost illegal to breathe too deeply without permission. His lessons on those countries reminded him of his talks with his professor. He had forgotten to say goodbye to her and now that he was in the CIA, she'd want to ask too many questions and he'd be too tempted to tell her, so he put the thoughts of seeing or calling her out of his mind. He didn't stop to think that it could be years before he would see his parents again after they left his college graduation. It was all exciting and new. He was a CIA agent, a spy.

Chapter Twelve

Over the years Jonathan had grown tired of pointless assignments where he had risked his life only to have policies change with the next President or Congress. He had grown tired of torture, the smell of death and the lack of the closeness of a family that he could talk to. With each new identity that he assumed and each new make-believe family, he knew not to like it too much or get too comfortable in that role.

Through it all he knew he had one true friend though. A friend he met on a joint training mission between U.S. agents and Britain's SIS, formerly known as M16. On leave, they would hang out, chase women and fight terrorism. Peter had become the brother he never had. Peter was from England. His mom was from South Africa and had settled in England and his dad was Irish. He was from a tough bunch. Having grown up with three older brothers and two older sisters he had to learn to fend for himself quickly. He told Jonathan that his dad had been a boxer but didn't involve him in boxing. Instead he signed him up for martial arts. Peter had served two terms in the military and two years in special service. For all but his first two years, he was a helicopter pilot.

Jonathan had become proficient in Tae Kwon Do, but Peter had been training since a child and had studied both Tae Kwon Do and Kung Fu. It was evident how good he was when watching him spar with other agents during their training together. He rarely lost, while Jonathan could hold his own. Jonathan's proficiency was in weapons. He loved guns. Guns of all types and calibers. Rifles, handguns, both semi and fully automatic all became extensions of who he was while on a mission. There would be certain situations that would require certain guns. Peter was good in martial arts and could turn almost anything into a weapon and use it with lethal efficiency.

Peter had initially skipped college. At just a few months passed his eighteenth birthday, he joined the military to get out and to see the world. After being in the military a few years, Peter grew tired of being a grunt and decided that he wanted to be a pilot; he enrolled in college and after graduating he enrolled in flight school. Jonathan knew that having a helicopter pilot as a good friend meant that he'd feel a lot better about flying out on a mission.

Chapter Thirteen

Jonathan and Peter had met on various missions over the years. It was the first time they had seen each other again since their joint mission in Brazil. This time, they were sent to Paris to begin an assignment on tracking terrorists in Sudan. Both of their agencies had been watching the leader of Al Qaeda, a man named Osama Bin Laden. They would meet for a short briefing and planning session in Paris and then travel to Sudan. Once in Sudan, they would be briefed and then taken out with a Sudanese contingency that knew the area.

Although he had grown up in Germany, Jonathan had never been to France. It wasn't that he hadn't wanted to visit; he just never had the opportunity. All of the joint international agencies would be meeting the next day at the Directorate General for External Security's (DGSE) building not far from the hotel where he, Peter and agents from other foreign countries were staying. Jonathan's favorite part of the job had always been the travel and learning something new about other cultures.

The morning he arrived in Paris, Jonathan took a taxi to Hotel Duo on Rue du Tempe which was only a few blocks south of the DSGE building. After checking into his room he decided to go to the lobby and possibly for a walk to get a feel for France. His French was a little weak, but he'd make do along the way. There wasn't much going on in the lobby. He decided to walk up Rue Du Temple. Peter wouldn't be arriving until later that afternoon.

An assortment of small cars and mini-vans lined the street on the right and stands of bicycles and small motorcycles were on the left of the narrow road. Paris wasn't much different from Germany. The buildings looked old on the outside. Most were. Inside, they were very modern, giving a person the feeling that he had left one century and entered another just from walking in from outside. It was a little cool that morning and many of the people up early were wearing light coats and jeans. About a block away from the hotel, Jonathan decided to go into a small store called RS Accessories, a grocery store selling import items along with snacks and other grocery items.

"Bonjour, Monsieur. Comment allez-vous?" Asked the Asian store clerk that greeted him as he entered. "Je suis très bien. Vous remercie de poser. J'ai juste pensé que je serais ramasser quelques choses pour la chambre." "Oh," she said in English with only a slight Vietnamese accent. "You're looking for toiletries for the visit here. You must be staying at Hotel Duo down the street. You're a business man?" Jonathan said "Yes". He knew that she was being nosy. Not just by asking him if he was a businessman, but by asking in

English. She really wanted to know his nationality. With the hotel being so close to DGSE, she must have sold toiletries to every spy in the world…literally. Jonathan moved along, browsing through snacks he might want to eat later that evening.

Jonathan spent the rest of the day in his room going over his notes for the mission. They would be moving into an area already secured by the Sudanese government and it was above the enemy camp just a little over a mile away. The Sudanese camp had a dual purpose; it really was a mineral mining camp but it was also used to survey the activities going in the mountains. At about 6:30 that evening the phone on the nightstand rang. He picked it up. "Hello, Jonathan. Peter here. I'm in my room. Let's meet down in the Pub in a few minutes."

Same old Peter, Jonathan thought. This is going to be an interesting trip. "Sure, I'll see you in a few." He then locked his notes inside the room safe. On each mission, the Agency always recommended to field agents which hotel to stay. Not much was left to chance. The background of every hotel staff member had been researched and the hotel's security was reviewed. Everyone knew hotels near a meeting site would be teaming with agents for sometimes up to a month. Even the store clerk had figured this out by now. The agency knew this would be the case and didn't take chances on losing secrets or an agent, especially not secrets; agents could be replaced on a college career day.

Jonathan never worried about an intruder or hotel staffer going through or stealing anything from his room. It was the CIA that worried him more than anything. It was the CIA that would plant a bug or rifle through his papers while he was gone to make sure he hadn't turned on them. He was sure that Peter was in his room doing the same thing he was. To not do so was a mistake that only rookies made. Jonathan had seen what the agency could do, and sometimes did to an agent they felt could no longer be trusted. Agents vanished off the face of the earth, or after the Agency finished destroying their life and career…most of them had found that it was easier to put a bullet through their own head.

Jonathan went down to the hotel bar and had to wait only a few minutes before Peter showed up. The long-time pals hugged each other and ordered drinks. They spent the rest of the evening catching the other up on news since their last visit—the jokes about the close calls that they encountered and how they narrowly escaped with their lives. By the time they said good night, the bar was about to close and each of them had a few drinks too many. For the next two days they stayed isolated, only venturing to each other's room to discuss details of the mission and to make sure not to miss anything, hoping that the other would catch any mistakes before some Arab with an AK-47 or RPG realized they made one.

On Monday morning, the alarms rang at the same time for both men. They were instructed to walk the few blocks north to their meeting place. They left the hotel dressed casually, looking more like college students than as spies and trained mercenaries of Western society. They leisurely walked up the street talking about anything except the real reasons they were there. When they got to the address, the sign above the door said CGI Imports. They opened the door and saw what any customer off the street would see in an import shop—merchandise and a clerk sitting behind the counter waiting for customers.

When the man heard the doorbell ring he put down his newspaper, stood up and straightened his ill-fitting eye-glasses. The man asked, "Bonjour. Que puis-je vous vendre gentlemen?" Jonathan responded, "I don't speak much French, but I'm looking to buy a camera." Those were the magic words that would let the man know he was to show them to the stairs in the room behind the counter. The man looked them over for a moment and decided that he didn't need further verification. He opened the door and pointed to the stairs. "Go up those stairs. You'll be given further instructions when you go in." His French had been perfect, Jonathan thought, noticing that the man's true accent sounded like he was from Texas.

Jonathan and Peter went up the stairs to the second floor where they were greeted by a man that must have been nearing sixty, Jonathan guessed from seeing the gray hair, a few visible wrinkles worn into his leathery face and hands. Otherwise he was built as if he worked out several times a day. "Good morning Gentlemen," he said with a slight French accent. "Welcome to your first day at DGSE. We won't be selling you any cameras today." Jonathan wondered about that and almost asked what would they did if a real customer came to buy a camera. How did the man downstairs know the difference? He decided against asking. He didn't know how this guy would take his sarcasm.

"We've got some refreshments on the table there. Some rolls and other things there in case you haven't eaten." After you've helped yourself, we'll begin." This same routine went on every other day. They were asked to skip a day and stay at the hotel for surveillance of any suspicious people and to make sure they were not followed. On those days Jonathan and Peter would casually observe to see if they had seen a face more than once in or around the hotel. On their next visit to the shop two Arab men were already in the room with their instructor. Peter and Jonathan nodded hello to the men and took a seat next to them.

Their instructor introduced the men. "Peter, Jonathan. I would like for you to meet Azad and Fadil. These gentlemen will be assigned with you for obvious reasons. Although both of you are fluent in Arabic, there may be some things that you may be able to learn from Azad and Fadil. They are good men and if there is ever any doubt about anything or if you see something that looks a little bit curious or out of sorts, talk with them about it. It could save your lives; otherwise it would mean we'd have to train someone else and that would set us behind on our mission now wouldn't it?" Jonathan admired his instructor's dry and pragmatic sense of humor.

Of course he didn't want to lose an agent, but the reality of it was that he was telling the truth. Azad and Fadil had arrived the night before and were also at Hotel Duo. After meeting for several hours discussing the movements of the people that they were tracking in Sudan, they quit for the day. The four men walked back to the hotel together, making small talk along the way, looking in shop windows and flirting with women on the street. *These guys are going to be a lot of fun*

Jonathan thought. At the hotel, they all decided to have lunch together.

"So where are you guys from?" Peter asked. "We are from all over, just like you. I was born in Yemen and Fadil is from Egypt. What about you guys?" Azad asked. Peter responded. "I'm from England." Jonathan said, "I was born in Germany, my father was in the military, but I'm an American. Which agency are you guys from?" Peter asked. "We're with Mossad." Fadil stated, "That's Israeli. Pretty good agency." "Yes, it is. It may seem odd, but not all Arabs hate Jews. It's a misconception. There are those radical leaders in the Middle East who preach hatred for their own power and then screw their people. There are people like Fadil and I who don't want this. We need to end this conflict before we destroy the world; what good would that do?" "Are you Muslim?" Peter asked. "No, we are Christians," he said. "We are all children of the same God," Azad added. "All countries have great opportunities for its people, but through greed and corruption, those opportunities are squandered and who suffers? It's the people." "You're right Azad," Peter said. "I've seen the same problem all over the world."

"The people get screwed over. It's the politicians that are the problem, but not just them. Surprisingly, it's also the churches and religions of the world that are causing more problems than they solve, all in the name of God." Jonathan and Fadil agreed with him. "I was in Africa not too long ago," Fadil added. "You wouldn't believe the conditions there for the people." "The leaders live very well. Everybody else lives like shit." Jonathan said. "And here we sit. We'll be going on another mission here in a few days to supposedly help. Help what? Our reports probably won't even get read." All agreed. Azad asked the group, "Have you guys ever heard of the Knights Templar?" He continued before they answered.

"The Knights Templar had a reputation of doing some very bad things to accomplish what the Catholic Church saw as being right. Who knew if it was or not? Over two centuries later, the Muslims and Christians are still at war. In a way, we're like modern- day knights. We're gladiators and we kill or be killed for the sake of our Kingdoms." With that, Jonathan asked for the check and they all decided to go to their rooms and relax for a few hours. They agreed to continue the conversation later that evening over dinner. Jonathan entered his room, turned on the television, and plopped down on the bed. The conversation with Fadil and Azad brought back memories of the discussions he had had with his college professor, Fahima. *She was a beautiful person,* Jonathan thought. *What had their conversations during those days of his learning gotten him into?*

The Sudanese 144th Counter Terrorist Unit had been receiving information on terrorist activity in Sudan since 1991. Their secret agency had been investigating Osama Bin Laden since his arrival there. The United States wanted no part of it because of the concerns of people back home and their sympathy for the killings in Darfur currently in the headlines. The President didn't want him to be arrested and brought back to the United States for a trial. The Saudis didn't want him either. Bin Laden had become an international hot potato that no one wanted to touch. DGSE had decided to get some eyes there on the ground. They couldn't believe that the United States would play so fast and loose with such a dangerous threat.

After being turned down to turn over the information that had been accumulated on Bin Laden and at least three hundred of his followers, the Sudanese government turned it over to the DGSE. The information was accurate as far as they could tell, but a closer look was going to be needed. The Sudanese had done their homework but it still needed to be confirmed by their own agents. DGSE contacted England and the United States so they could include those two nations, and in their own eyes and ears learn what was necessary for their own comfort level with the information. All indications were that Osama Bin Laden was a serious threat. So, here he was.

Nearly a week had gone by and Peter and Jonathan were getting restless being chained to their hotel rooms. That morning as they were seated in the hotel lobby, eating breakfast, Azad and Fadil joined them and told them that the group would be leaving the next morning. "How did you find out?" Peter asked. "The old man, the instructor—he called us."

The next morning, they were at the airport preparing to leave on the approximately four-hour flight to Sudan. The four agents knew that air travel to Sudan would be a hair-raising adventure because of their airlines safety records and they were right. The flight over had been like being strapped to a bull and holding on. Jonathan remembered helicopter rides that were straining at the altitudes in Afghanistan that had been smoother than this hop. The plane was old and the pilot didn't look much younger. Peter was a pilot himself and after looking over at him, Jonathan saw the look of a man that wanted to touch the ground again.

The plane was crowded and the flight was choppy and jerky. It lasted a little longer than expected and Jonathan was thankful that the trip was finally over. After arriving and picking up their suitcases they headed for the Corinthian Hotel, which was only a few minutes' drive from the Sudan National Intelligence and Security Service office. Their meeting with agents from the NISS would be the next morning. The men all retired to their rooms to review notes on what would be covered the next morning. From there they would go on to interrogate terrorists that had been captured during various ground operations, if they were still conscious and able to speak at the time. Sudan was one of those nations that had no problems with torturing a prisoner. Some of the methods were encouraging prisoners to speak by threatening rape, putting a paper bag full of chili-powder over captive's heads, or using their testicles to put out cigarettes. These methods would either make a captive talk, die or live a very fragile life, if ever released. The alarm went off at nearly the same time in the four men's rooms. After dressing and meeting in the lobby, they hailed a taxi to the NCISS building.

After a short ride, they entered and were taken down several halls into a conference room of sorts. The receptionist left them and they waited for a few minutes before the man they were to meet, came in carrying an arm full of three-ring binders. "Good morning gentlemen. I'm Mr. Zarede. Sorry to have kept you waiting for so long. Have you had something to eat or drink this morning? If not, we'll order something for you. We're going to have a long day here, since there is a lot of information for us to go over," he said.

Mr. Zarede gave them a tour of the facility after lunch that day. He seemed to get a special joy from his job that seemed a little sadistic to Jonathan and he wasn't sure if that was a good thing or not. He had seen agents in the CIA with the same mentality; they enjoyed causing pain and misery on those over which they held power. To Jonathan, it was a job that needed to be done and nothing in which to take joy or pride. After all, he thought, they made bad choices and they would pay for those choices, He was a firm believer himself in justice, just not sadism. Mr. Zarede escorted them to the prisoner section. The Sudanese had used a big portion of their oil proceeds to have a state-of-the-art facility.

Each cell's ceiling was made of two-way, hardened glass. They had to take a flight of stairs to get to the catwalk that made up the ceiling of each cell. From this vantage point, a guard could see everything the prisoner was doing from above. In one cell a prisoner was being interrogated by two men. Thankfully, the glass muffled his screams as they tortured him mercilessly. In other cells, men were sleeping, using the bathroom or looking up as if they knew that someone was watching them. The brain was a funny thing. Sometimes instincts would kick in out of the blue and at other times people would miss things that were right in front of them.

Did these men instinctively know they were being watched through the two way glass, or were they just trying to figure out how to break it without killing themselves with a ton of glass falling in on them? Mr. Zarede gave the men a status report on each of the prisoners that had been brought in for terrorism either in Sudan or other parts of the world that couldn't afford to be caught torturing prisoners. Over the next few days, they spent most of the day asking captured combatants' questions.

Those who didn't answer would be turned back over to the men who'd been torturing them that evening. Those who did talk were given a trip to the medical facility and then held until they were strong enough to be tortured again without dying. Eventually, most would die and then be tossed into a nameless grave somewhere. Wherever they were from, they'd never see it again and their families would be left to wonder to where they disappeared. Mr. Zadere had planned their field expedition to go out and observe terrorist training camps where Bin Laden was reported seen recently.

The day arrived and Sudanese soldiers accompanied them. The total count was fourteen; this would allow them to stand ground against any attack on the camp until air support was called. Then it wouldn't be much of a fight at all. The Sudanese soldiers wore standard gear for their army. Jonathan and his men were in desert camouflage. Each of them had packed their favorite guns. Each had a rifle and handgun that worked for them. Guns and ammo would be pretty much all they'd need. They didn't need an interpreter, sleeping bags, explosives or any of the other gear they'd brought. Fadil was a radio operator and he'd be taking communications equipment to coordinate with the Sudanese and call for air support from choppers in the area, if needed. The Sudanese already had an outpost overlooking the camp. They were mining for something or another, so they'd be staying in one of the tents set up for them. They'd be sleeping on the ground, and have a little cover from the cold. The outposts also had a mess hall and an around-the-clock detail patrolling the perimeter—at least they would have a somewhat decent meal. They would be dropped into a zone several miles from the outpost further up the mountain and then work their way down to the camp. They would then observe the training facilities with field glasses and Fadil would try to pick up a frequency on them. A lot of the stuff they'd be doing could be observed from a satellite but those were not the same as being there. *Human intelligence is always better than a machine*, Jonathan thought to himself. Mr. Zadere wanted to kill two birds with one stone that day. He was sending one of their best sharpshooters along to take out several targets that day. He never mentioned what offenses these targets had committed against the Sudanese government or why they would be killed. Bin Laden wasn't going to be one of them.

Some things in the spy business were best left unsaid so Jonathan and his contingency asked no questions. "Gentlemen, please radio me when you have had your fill of studying that training facility; our men will show you how to get to the next. Take as long as you want. If you get into trouble please radio for support and it will be made quickly available. If you don't have any questions then let's go." With that said, the men were off. The helicopter ride to the drop spot was almost an hour. The helicopter had moaned and groaned all the way up the mountain. They were not designed to try to climb to the altitudes in which they were often forced to navigate. None of the men talked much as they approached the drop spot. They'd be exiting the copter by rope from about a hundred feet up. Hopefully, no one would break a leg on the ground. When the last man slipped down and reached the ground, Jonathan quickly assessed everyone and then gave the go ahead to start the two-mile walk of descent to the outpost. They were there to defend their Western nations and put their own safety aside, once again. Darkness was only a few hours away. They would be getting to the outpost at nightfall. Besides the occasional bursts of machine gunfire from the camps and an off-target mortar fired in the camp's general direction that was rarely even close, there wasn't much of a real danger to the camp because of its location, even with the high value target of Bin Laden. It seemed that they knew that no one wanted Osama as a captive and by the freak chance that he was wounded instead of killed, they would have to bring him in. If he was killed, they would have a real threat. Bin Laden would become a martyr and there would easily be more people stepping in to fill his shoes. No, they needed Bin Laden alive…at least for now. All they were doing was really meaningless. It was just politicians making themselves look good in case a reporter came along and tried to make a name for himself. The powers in the government could say they were trying. They had to at least make it look good. Jonathan and the men accompanying him were extras on their movie set. Nothing was real and men died every day because of this game. He would do his job, play his role, but he wasn't going to die for it. Not today. Not any day. It was always best to travel under the cover of darkness.

The Sudanese soldiers were leading the way as they kicked up dust. After about thirty minutes, they stopped. The lead guy gave the halt signal to those behind them. Then he stopped again. He asked Peter and Jonathan to follow him towards the side of the trail.

"That is something new that terrorists are doing, my friends." He said. "It is an IED, an Improvised Explosive Device. A bomb," he continued. "I will send one of our men trained in explosives and demolition to disarm it." You stay here." With that he went to one of the men in the rear.

One soldier followed him back. "This is our expert." The young soldier went towards the device, worked to find its frequency and then exploded it. The soldier must not have done this too often. He was standing too close to the device and was killed immediately. He had underestimated the size of the handmade bomb. The shockwave knocked the Sudanese officer, as well as Jonathan and Peter to the ground and when they got up, their ears were ringing. "Fuck, a little warning would have been nice," Peter screamed.

Jonathan was sure that the explosion was heard for miles. Jonathan's rank put him in charge of this group of now thirteen men. He would need to get advice about the terrain from the senior officer, but this was his mission from here out. After spending nearly a month with Peter, Azad and Fadil they all knew what Jonathan was capable of. The device that just exploded triggered by a cell phone was pretty creative considering that the cell phone was not in wide-spread use here and typically was only used by military personnel in these mountains. This meant this trap was set to kill military. But why was there no firefight afterwards? There were no call towers up here. This had been a set up, but by whom and why?

This new war on terror was going to be a learning experience. There had already been an explosion and one man killed. Jonathan was going to do his best to keep his men safe but who could know for sure. However, it didn't stop him from being mad about the incident. The contingent continued south towards Khartoum North until the road started a gradual turn towards the northwest where the roads faded into a more rocky and hilly terrain.

They were heading towards a mountainous region where they could observe the training facilities, hopefully without anyone spotting them. Peter had remained pretty quiet during the whole process. They all had. It was starting to dawn on them just how much the world was in trouble. There was so much hatred that one part of humanity had for the other. How cruel life could be for no apparent reason. All of them had seen death up close and personal. Peter and Jonathan had both grown up in Western nations. They didn't realize the constant underlying currents that bubbled up from just beneath the surface.

Jonathan's mother had been too young to experience the evils of Hitler, but she often relayed stories to Jonathan about him, stories that had been passed down from his grandparents. Like many nations, the soil of Germany had been fertilized with the blood of soldiers who fought battles over land, religion, pride and money. *Why should things be different now?* he asked himself? The appearance of civility and the changes in technology hid the fact that men were still the same warriors as they had been for centuries.

As they approached their destination, the Sudanese soldiers slowed at a guard station. It blocked the road that led to their spot on the mountain to view the training camps. This region was chosen because of its proximity to the pristine wells that sprang up from the oasis nearby. The camps were located in the center of a valley that gave the men the feeling of security. They did not think anyone knew that they were there and they could see people come from the distance. They also had outposts.

They had to realize that there was no such thing since most modern nations had satellites that could show how many buttons they had on their shirts and missiles that could zero in on any one of those buttons from miles away. Jonathan knew as an insider that soon there would be unmanned electric aircrafts that could silently fly near this camp and kill them all before they could see what was coming. Jonathan knew that within years, missions like this would be unnecessary to officials in Washington, who were always concerned about the public's opinion of an American death.

Anytime an American died in action, certain sections of society who were anti-war would scream and demand that men be brought home. Little did they realize or care that those lives were given voluntarily because those soldiers didn't mind dying so that their families back home could stay free. There had been too many wars, too many soldiers' lives needlessly wasted and too many battles that had brought about too many deaths only to be ended right before a complete victory could be claimed. That was when the deaths of these men and women became hollow and pointless.

It was only when politics and politicians became personally involved in the war because of their need to hold on to their jobs that wars became a game to them— a game of real-life chess being played with no intentions of winning, but to only within a few moves of winning; knocking the board over and then starting over to knock it over again became the routine. Jonathan snapped back to the reality at hand. He touched the 9 mm in his holster to remind himself that it was there. He noticed Peter, who was walking beside him, do the same thing almost at the same time. That told him that his instincts about being stopped by guards on this road were not a good thing.

Funny how no one had had mentioned a roadblock during their training sessions. Then he saw the Jeep ahead move forward and the guard at the gate wave them through. Who was this guard? Whose side was he on? Questions that at this point didn't matter as much as being allowed to walk through the gate and not have to kill someone or be killed somewhere on a mountain road in Sudan. "Peter," he turned to his friend and said, "If we get through this, we're going to have to go out and have a drink." Peter replied, "Sure thing Jonathan; wouldn't have it any other way. We'll take along our new friends back there, Azad and Fadil. They seem to be some pretty good blokes."

The men arrived at the spot the Sudanese had used before. They unpacked their gear and Jonathan walked over to the sergeant that had given the orders for the young soldier to die and almost get them killed and said, "That young man back there that was killed was strike one with me. Strike two was not being informed about the guards at the road block. From now on, I want you to tell me if you need to take a piss. Am I clear?" Any defiance that the man may have felt wasn't shown. He tried to explain, "Sir, I did not stop to think that such matters of small importance would upset you. Look around sir."

Jonathan hadn't taken the time to notice the base camp and what looked like preparations for a mining operation. "What is this?" Jonathan asked.

It is our cover sir. We opened this operation up shortly after the terrorists moved in. They know we are here. They don't know that our government minds that they are here. We've made sure that they've gotten word that we are conducting exploratory drilling here. "Drilling for what? Jonathan shot back.

"Whatever sir. They never asked. It could be anything. They have no suspicions of us. We are Muslims and they are Muslims. There is an inherent trust there."

"What about the man back there?"

"Sir, he was at one time one of them."

"What do you mean, he was one of them?" Jonathan asked.

"Well sir, he used to be a terrorist and he came over to us. We found out that he was insincere and he was about to go back and reveal what he had learned about us."

Jonathan looked at him, but did not respond. "You're dismissed Sergeant." There were two reasons that Jonathan didn't respond. One it was protocol not to get involved or speak against an agency's 'housekeeping'. The other was the lingering question of what was the real reason for bringing them here—to have a cover for an operation that was unknown to them, or to have one of his team members eliminated. In this line of work one was never sure.

This small group of men stayed for several days on the mountain, observing the activities below. They saw a tall man almost certainly Bin Laden with an entourage around him. They saw the adoration of his followers as he walked through the facility. Obviously he was there on a tour. He obviously knew the importance of making an appearance, although it was a low-key appearance not filled with ticker-tape and limousines. After his visit and discussions with small groups of men at a time, he left with his guards, who were carrying semi-automatic rifles.

Once Bin Laden left, the men continued their training—hand-to-hand combat, shooting at lifeless targets and blowing things up. It seemed that blowing up things was one of their favorite activities. After days of observation, days of being plied with information beforehand in preparation of this exploratory trip, Jonathan, Peter, Azad and Fadil had seen and heard enough to make their reports to their respective agencies. It was time to go home. Before going home, they needed to stop over in Paris and report back to DGSE. They all agreed that they'd spend a few days in Paris, sight-seeing, relaxing and blowing off some steam before leaving for their homes. After they arrived back in Paris, Jonathan and Peter called from their secure satellite phones to see if the reports had been received and if there would be further actions needed.

Each agency told them their reports had been filed for future reference and no further action was needed on this assignment. They both knew what that meant. It meant that their reports would never see the light of day. It meant that someone higher up had decided not to use the Intel for political reasons. It meant that the planning, the money and the danger that they had just gone through didn't matter to anyone. *What the hell*, he thought, *time to get drunk.* He called Peter, Azad and Fadil and said, "Hey guys. Let's go have some fun while we're here in Paris. Drinks are on me. Let's meet in the bar downstairs in an hour and go from there." As planned, they met in the bar an hour later.

Chapter Fourteen

After the first few drinks, talk turned to work as it usually does when men are in bars. If not women or sports, work is usually a safe topic, even for spies on the road and a long way from home. "Guys, I'm really pissed. This isn't the first time that I've risked my life for a cause and my country. Probably won't be the last, but damn. What will it take for them to wake up? This guy Bin Laden is training idiots in the desert. I mean hundreds of them…with a new batch almost every day. What does our government think that this is about?" Jonathan complained.

"Well Jonathan, old pal. We are the low men on the totem pole. Shit slides downhill and falls on us. When we climb up that slippery pole then some poor old bloke will be the recipient of our shit," said Azad. The discussion went on for about thirty-minutes when Azad said, "Hey look, we've got a few days here. Fadil and I have months of vacation time. How about you guys? Can you take some time off?"

Peter and Jonathan both decided it might not be such a bad idea to take a break and clear this mission and their anger at their agencies and politicians out of their heads. Jonathan asked, "What did you have in mind Azad?" Azad told him, "I was thinking about going to Amsterdam. I've got a friend here in Paris that has a car. We don't have to rent anything. He's a car dealer and we can go get something off the lot and drive for him. We'll be doing him a favor." The guys agreed to leave the next morning. It was time for some rest so they all headed for their rooms.

It all started for Jonathan with one phone call. "Hello." Jonathan answered. There was a brief silence. Then the man on the other end of the call said, "Hello Jonathan. You don't know me and you probably never will. We may talk from time to time, but even that will be on an as-needed basis." Jonathan tried to shake the sleep from his head. How did this person get his number for a secure satellite phone? Who had the balls to call a CIA agent and be mysterious? Was this some sort of joke from one of the guys back at headquarters? No, even they didn't have his number and he didn't have any of theirs. He would receive weekly calls from the agency with codes to all agents' phones. Each week, the codes would change in case an agent lost a phone. "Jonathan, let's get to the point of my call. But first let me ask you if know anything about history. The Knights Templar to be specific?"

"Who the hell is this?" Jonathan demanded as if he'd really get an answer to the question.

"Jonathan, you've done quite a few assignments in your career with the CIA. I won't get into specifics, but let's just say your last assignment was meant to get rid of you and your friend Peter. You were not supposed to make it out alive. As I was saying, you have been on many missions and you now know a bit too much for their liking. But don't worry. They don't know who really brought you to your mission. They thought it was the DGSE...well it was and it wasn't." He had gotten Jonathan's attention. Jonathan knew the guy knew just what he was talking about, "Okay, I'm listening." Jonathan said. He still didn't know how to read this. Was this someone from the CIA? If it was, were they just playing mind games with him? The caller said, "This call is safe so your bosses at the CIA can't hear any of this. We brought you here and you met Azad and Fadil. Don't worry. They're good guys." Jonathan interrupted him, "How do I know you're telling the truth about any of this?" "Don't worry; I'm getting to that Jonathan," The caller continued. "The Knights Templar were defenders of Christians who were being persecuted and killed during the Medieval Period. The Knights were formed to protect those Christians who lived in what they call the Middle East now go on religious pilgrimages. They were constantly attacked and killed by Muslims. I won't bore you with all of the details. I'm just saying the Knights never died. If they did it was just for a short period and they were resurrected and evolved. That's who we are, Jonathan. We're the Knights Templar. We are the Knight family. When you and Peter spoke with Azad and Fadil last night, you admitted the truth. You know that governments do nothing but use people and throw them away. We've been watching the two of you for some time now. You're both good men Jonathan. You're not only good and honest people with good moral character, but you're good agents. When it came to our attention that you were to be sacrificed, we decided to run interference. So, you have a choice. You can hang up and go forward with your fate, or you can join forces with us fighting for the values of what Western nations should be. You can fight to defend our principles and faith, or you can go back to the CIA and spend the rest of your life trying to save it from a CIA who someday will kill you. I'll give you time to discuss this with your friend Peter tonight. I'll call you back at the same time tomorrow. If you contact anyone, I'll know. They won't ever find me…but you must understand that the deal I'm offering won't be on the table anymore and the two of you will be on your own." With that said, he hung up. Jonathan had no intention of going to Azad and Fadil. He knew that if he said the wrong thing to them it would get back to the guy that had just called. He wasn't sure of anything anymore. Over the years, he had been so groomed to be a spy that there wasn't much that confused him. This call did. He had to talk to Peter. He picked up the hotel room phone and dialed Peter's extension. Peter answered. "Hey Peter, I've got to talk to you. Not here in the hotel; we need to go for a walk." The two men met in the lobby. They decided to be safe and talk outside where Jonathan told Peter about the call he had received. "Jonathan, I believe the bloke. I've had that feeling since I got on this trip." Peter said. "I mean think about it. We've both seen it happen to other agents. What makes us so special to either of our governments? Sure, they've spent millions on training us…but it's not their money. It's the taxpayers' and they don't even know or care about where that money goes. I think we should have a little talk with Azad and Fadil before we make a decision. By the way…did they mention how much they're paying? How much does one get to outsmart his own government? I think that's priceless." Jonathan felt lighter. "Priceless? Cool, that means you don't mind if I take your share," he joked. If the guy calls back tell him we are considering his offer and we will talk more to Azad and Fadil about it."

The governments that sent them on assignments were sometimes aware of the existence of the Knight family; sometimes they weren't. Some governments never knew what had become of their agents. Back home parents would be notified about the death of their child.

When the dreaded knock on the door by two military officers came, they knew. It was a day they knew might come but hoped never would. Whether their child was actually dead or not wasn't the issue. They just knew that they would never see them again. They often hoped that their suspicions were right and their child was still alive since a body often was never recovered.

The next day, Jonathan, Peter, Azad and Fadil requested a few months off. Such a request was not frowned upon after an agent had just finished a long-term mission as long as they had accumulated the vacation time needed and asked for a break in action. As long as there was no immediate need for them, nine times out of ten it would be granted. Around noon, they took a taxi over to see Azad's friend. He greeted them at the door of the small building on the car lot. He was happy to see Azad and invited them all in. "Hey, Sammy. These are my friends. Peter, Jonathan and Fadil. We're here working and need to borrow a car."

"You name it Azad. Go see what's on the lot and come back and tell me which one. Then I'll give you the keys. Just don't drive too fast or wreck it." Azad had seen a black Mercedes that interested him even before greeting Sammy. The four of them went outside and Azad went straight to it. It looked like he had made up his mind. The other three men didn't get a vote, not that it made any difference.

"Hey, Fadil and I have another group of friends in Amsterdam. When we get there, I'd like for you to meet them. They are great guys. They are also spies like us. You'll be safe. We'll go out. They'll know the places that are hot. It's been awhile since I've been to Amsterdam. These clubs change owner's a lot and the crowd never stays in the same place for long. I want the place with the hottest ladies." Peter and Jonathan agreed. With that said, their next destination was Amsterdam, which was several hours away.

The conversation along the way was occasionally interrupted by Azad turning up the radio and singing along with whatever song that he heard and was familiar with. Finally, about half way through the trip, he turned the radio off and turned to Jonathan, who was sitting in the front seat. "Jonathan," he said. "You know that Fadil and I are with the Israeli secret agency and we are, but about five years ago, we got frustrated just like you and Peter are now. Even Israeli politicians are forced to make decisions that are not always in their best interest because of pressure from many things like the citizens or other nations. The list is long. Fadil and I both felt the same way. One day, we were introduced to some people. I know this will sound weird to you, but the Knights Templar are still alive. We never finished our conversation about the Knights Templar the last time we spoke about them.

Some say it is a fairly new organization; others say it has carried on. I don't know which one. I just know that Fadil and I joined about five years ago. We both talked about how much we can do working with them. We can do things that make a difference." Jonathan looked at him and asked, "Why are you telling me this Azad?"

"Because I noticed how frustrated you've been these past few days. I truly wanted you and Peter to have some fun and if this type of thing doesn't interest you, I'll never bring it up again in life."

"I'm listening," Jonathan said. He now knew the phone call was real.

Peter poked his head up from the backseat and was now in between the two head rests and said, "Yeah, me too." Fadil woke up from a nap and squeezed in to hear what was being discussed. "Jonathan, you and Peter are good men. Fadil and I talked about you back in Paris. We both thought the two of you would be a good addition. I mean what future do you have with the CIA? Look at this last assignment. It was a complete waste of time for you guys. You risk your life for more than just a check. I know I do. I want to make a difference and for once we are."

"How are you making a difference Azad?" Peter wanted to know. Instead, Fadil answered, "We live in Israel. We don't have a choice. Western nations have the luxury of being able to ignore a problem or get it wrong. Israel can't afford to get it wrong once. So far, God has been with us." Jonathan could tell they were sincere. "So tell me why we should trust that you guys are serious and if we did take you up on this, what about our jobs?" he asked.

Azad replied, "We still have our jobs with Mossad. However, they don't know and they won't. None of us have desk jobs or have to punch a clock. We're only called when needed. The Knights Organization does the same thing."

Peter laughed. "The Knights Organization? Are you serious? That organization died off years ago. Did they start a new one?"

It was starting to make sense now. The call was real. Azad and Fadil just confirmed it.

Fadil responded, "We're not sure. We were told that it's the original group. I mean not the same group of people but you know, the same Organization. The same money that comes from the same types of people. The Knights are funded not just by the Catholic Church now though. I've been told that we're funded by wealthy investors who care about Western interests. Maybe they are descendants of the original knights. The ones who left and hid somewhere a fortune and the Holy Grail. They know we are in a Holy War. A battle for the souls of the world. I'm not sure that if it's their souls or not...losing their money may be what they're worried about but I don't care. I care more about what I'm worried about and that's the survival of our way of life."

Jonathan then asked, "Then if you think that's how they think about things, what makes them any different than our politicians and bosses who have to follow their instructions back at the Agency?"

"I'll tell you how Jonathan." After saying that, Azad who was still tearing along the highway towards Amsterdam, reached into his back pocket with one hand and pulled out his wallet. He then found an emerald-colored credit card and handed it to Jonathan. "What's this?" Jonathan asked.

"What does it look like Jonathan? It's my credit card. Look at the name." The card read "Azad Knight." "The thing you can't see is that the card doesn't have a limit. Would your agency trust you with a card with no limit on how much you can spend? Wait, I'll answer for you; hell no they wouldn't." With his head still between the headrests, Peter jokingly said, "I'm in."

Jonathan was more reluctant; he had some questions but he was interested. *After all*, he thought. I *lie about who*

I am daily. what would one more lie be? If Fadil and Azad were lying to him, it wouldn't take him long to find out. "Before I make a commitment to an organization that does not have a very good track record I need to know more."

Azad pulled out two more credit cards. They each had already been printed with Peter and Jonathan's names on them. However, the last name on both was Knight. Azad handed them the cards and said, "No one really knows how much money is in the Knights' bank account for us to use; we just know it is unlimited. The investors really don't want to know where the money is going. Not knowing is a way to deny involvement. Muslims, Communists and others have their own streams of money being funneled similarly into such accounts where wealthy benefactors from around the world deposited money that would eventually lead to accounts that would then be used by those dedicated to furthering their causes. For Muslims, that cause is Mohammed and the advent of Sharia Law. For Christians in Western nations, the cause is Christianity, freedom and democracy. This same cause has divided the world since shortly after the death of Christ. The Knights Templar fought the same battle with Muslims centuries before and now it is us who carry the torch for Christians. Members of the Knight family are no saints. Sometimes people have to die to save others.

I am sorry to be so long-winded but I need to say all of this because we think you are good people."

Jonathan asked him why he had already had their names on the cards. "What if we say no?" "Easy," Azad replied. "You won't get the cards. You will go on with your lives with your Agency and we go on with ours. Now, if you're asked by someone in our family to help on an assignment, if you don't want to, you can say no. If you and Peter decide together or on your own that there is something else that needs to be addressed, you can work it alone or you can ask the Family for help. It will be up to you."

"One more question Azad," Peter said. "What if we just take these cards and disappear?"

Fadil answered. "Your card is just cancelled. I mean there are some limits you know. By the way, did I mention that there are some guys from the Family that I want you to meet in Amsterdam? We're going to stop by their house to talk for a few minutes and then we will all go out and have some fun."

Jonathan told him, "Hey, this is your mission. I'm just along for the ride." Azad replied, "You won't feel that way for long Jonathan. I'm sure that there will soon come a day when something really bugs you and you'll want to fix it. When that day comes, call us. I guess we're all part of the Knight Family now. We're all brothers." Peter chimed in, "Hurry up and get to Amsterdam Azad, so we can all have a drink to that."

All went well in Amsterdam. The four of them met several of their new family members and had a great time partying with them.

Once recruited as Knights, they knew what they needed to do. This shadowy group of agents was often mistaken for Black Ops, Special Forces and other teams by those who came into contact with them. Even their own governments did not question them as they officially did not exist.

Jonathan was trained as a Seal. He moved up to covert operations and assisted in some Black Op missions. In Black Op missions, the Government denies it has any involvement in the operation. Assassinations of foreign leaders, overthrowing governments and smuggling guns and drugs to rebels were the types of assignments that Black Ops received. Jonathan wasn't cut out for those types of unethical, illegal missions. They were too political and too dirty. The missions seemed to destroy more than they built. With the Knight family, he knew the mission had meaning—a meaning that might take a lifetime but saved many innocent lives and places where they lived.

Jonathan and Englishman Peter Donnelly had met on a mission. They had fought terrorists together in the mountains of Afghanistan.

Their mission was not just love of country; it was to help bring God's children back to his Kingdom and there were Knights that were willing to die for that. Some had died. Before they died, they were tortured. Women agents were tortured, raped, mutilated and then killed.

Jonathan and Peter attempted to rescue one of these captured female Knights from Muslims in Libya. Jonathan, Peter and three other Knights went in under the cover of darkness and stormed the compound but they were too late. There were still people at the compound who probably had nothing to do with the problem at hand but they were casualties of their raid just the same. In a battle, they did not have time to stop and interview each person to see who was guilty and who wasn't. They tried to be as quiet as they could while entering. They had been dropped in a few miles away from the target so the helicopters wouldn't be heard. Silencers were used to reduce the sounds of gunfire.

All of this was for nothing. The enemy had been gone for several hours. Their sister was killed, and abandoned. She had been tortured. It would have been nice to say her death was quick and painless, but it hadn't been. There were cigarette burns on her arms. She had been raped. Her breasts were mutilated and she had been shot in the head at close range. As Jonathan was going through the small houses in the compound trying to gather information, the other men were bagging up their fallen knight's body. There would be no military burial, no twenty-one-gun salute nor families in attendance. This woman would get an unceremonious and unmarked grave somewhere on a piece of land that the Knight Organization owned. There were no rewards for being a Knight who gave one's life for the cause. Her only consolation was she knew before she died that she was about to give her life back to her Creator and she would be in his care and a better place.

Experiences like these shaped Jonathan's outlook in life and his determination to make a difference even if it meant that he would have to put his life on the line. Johnathan was okay with that.

Chapter Fifteen

Over the years, both Peter and Jonathan kept their secret from others with the exception of a few other agents who were part of the family. They had been dual agents and conducted missions and interrogations with both their respective agencies and the Knight Family. Although separated by thousands of miles, the day that Azad had spoken of finally came for Jonathan and Peter on the same day—September 11, 2001. On that morning by chance, both men were not on assignment from the CIA or Ml-6. Peter was in his apartment in England where he normally stayed when there wasn't much going on.

He was watching TV when they interrupted the show with an emergency news bulletin showing a plane flying into the World Trade Center. On the night before, he was out with some friends shooting darts. He had a chance to go home with one the waitresses at the pub, but he hadn't been in the mood. All evening he had been preoccupied with his role as a Knight. It had been over five years and he had not experienced the life-changing mission that made joining any more rewarding than just working with Ml-6. He thought back to when he and Jonathan had been brought into the family and what Azad had said about joining the Knight family being a special and defining moment for them.

He watched his defining moment—a defining moment for not just him, but for people all over the world. It was pronounced when watching the second plane hit the other tower live on TV. Millions of people all over the world were watching. As the upper floors of the first building burned behind the second building, plane two flew in at five hundred miles an hour. Peter immediately knew that he had just witnessed those in the building, anywhere nearby and those in planes perishing before his eyes. He was dumbstruck. He knew it was an act of terrorism.

Within seconds his phone rang. It was Jonathan, whom he had not heard from for several months. "Peter," Jonathan said as he breathed hard into the phone. "Did you see it? Did you see what those assholes did to the towers? Screw our government Peter." He said, "We're going to get these bastards, and I'm not asking anyone's permission and I'm not writing a report after risking my life just to have someone throw it away." Peter could tell Jonathan had probably seen more than he had. "Were you up when the first plane hit?" Peter asked. "Yeah, I just watched the second plane hit. The people in the building never knew what hit them. Those trapped above the fire are going to have a hard time getting down from those heights," he said.

Jonathan was right; the wind and extreme heat from the flames would be too much for even a military chopper with the best pilot in the world. Those trapped above the flames would soon have a choice of being burned alive or jumping to their deaths. Even if they did decide to die in the flames, the pain and smell of their own burning flesh would probably cause them to jump, and many were doing just that as both men watched the same scene unfold from miles apart. "Jonathan, what did you have in mind? Whatever it is, I'm ready to go," Peter said. "Our world has just changed and nothing will ever be the same again. I'm not having this either Jon. If anyone can do something about it, who else would it be besides us? Besides the Knights. You're exactly right. Do you think it's Bin Laden?"

Jonathan didn't hesitate. "Yeah, I do." He said. "We had a chance to take him out back in Sudan and we weren't allowed to. But it's not just Bin Laden. If we get Bin Laden, there's a thousand more Bin Laden's that have been trained since we were in Sudan. No, the problem is much bigger. We're going after the people in the Middle East and in our own governments who've allowed this to happen when we could have stopped it five years ago." Peter agreed. "Where do we start? Are you off? I'm on vacation." Jonathan replied, "No, I'm not. I'm sure we'll be getting a call soon about the alert.

This is nothing like I have ever seen. They're locking everything down. I've been tinkering with some software for a few months now. I'm just about done. I was going to try to patent and sell it. I don't think I will now. I think I'll keep it for us. We'll need it now."

He went on to explain it to Peter. "We're going to need to communicate with each other more frequently and privately. The software will allow us to do that. Think of a submarine. It can operate both on the surface and underneath the water equally as well. We should be able to do the same with this. We can either chat on the surface or below where everything is encrypted and no one will know what's being said." Peter replied, "Cool. When will it be ready?"

Jonathan told him, "I need to test it. I'd say within two weeks. Stay close to your computer for the next few days if you can. We can start testing it today. I wasn't really in a hurry to get it done before now. Let's get it done. All hell's breaking loose and we're going to need to prepare. We are going to have to operate without any of our agencies knowing. After you and I test it, it's going to be my gift to the Knights and probably the world we're about to try to save from Armageddon." Peter saw the urgency, but Jonathan's last thought about Armageddon seemed a little extreme, but considering what had just happened to the Trade Centers he understood his emotion.

He thought for a minute. This all just happened so fast that he hadn't stopped to think of the people that he knew that worked there. "Hey Jonathan, I'll stay close to the computer. I just remembered, I've got friends that work in tower one. I need to check on them. I'm on board. I'll help however you need me. I'll call you later." Jonathan wasn't sure if he knew anyone there but he knew it wouldn't be a problem for him to get a list of passengers on the planes that had been hijacked as well as a list of those who worked in the towers. He didn't know yet that within several hours his list would include the Pentagon and a field in Pennsylvania.

"Okay Peter. I'm going to do the same. I don't think I know anyone but you never know. I'll get back to you this afternoon." Jonathan turned on his radio and scanners. He wanted to start monitoring the chatter from all sides. He logged on to his computer to start doing the same thing. He logged into the CIA site and began reading the communiqué between agencies around the world. This had caught most of them off guard completely and it shouldn't have. Now, everyone was trying to understand what he had tried to tell them five years earlier. He didn't feel like going down that rabbit hole and getting entangled with them. He decided to just monitor the situation.

He logged into his own site that he had just talked to Peter about and began working as the other cascade of information on the unfolding events swirled around him on his scanner and radio. Periodically, he'd check the CIA site to see if any of them yet had a clue. Just as he thought, his phone rang. It was his boss. "Jonathan, this is Greg from the office. I'm sure you're watching all of this." Jonathan replied, "Yes sir. I have the television, scanner, radio and just logged into our home site." Greg asked him, "What do you know about this, anything?"

Again, Jonathan reminded himself not to get pulled too deeply into their mess. He knew after all of these years now that it would be pointless, so he said, "Yes, sir just a little. What I know about it is in my reports starting back in Sudan. I think I have a total of eight reports. Each detailing probably whose responsible Sir. I haven't checked the flight list yet to see who's on there, but at least one of my reports may include the drivers, Sir." His boss sighed and asked him, "Why the hell didn't you tell someone Jonathan? Let me go find those reports and go through them. I'll call you later. Stay on alert. I may have some questions for you after I read them." He hung up.

Typical, Jonathan thought. He had been one of several agents who had been trying to warn his bosses at the CIA for years, who had always been less concerned about the possibility of what happened today than kissing up to the politicians who made the final call on any of their missions. He left his work open and switched to tracking down the flight lists. When he did he started pouring over them to see if he recognized any of the names. He did, but also found a person whom he did not expect to find there—his college professor, the beautiful Arab woman that had taught him so much about languages and life in the coffee shops they used to visit and talk for hours.

She had been on the first plane. It seemed that her father's desire to bring her to America and the safety and freedom for her from the brutality of living in Saudi Arabia had come full circle and they had unintentionally found her and punished her for the perceived sins of her father. She had been one of the first to die this morning. Her death would not be forgotten as Jonathan filled with rage and his eyes with tears.

Jonathan sent Peter a message to his email. "Hi Peter, this is Jonathan. Please click the attached link. When you get into the first page of the program, it will automatically begin downloading. Leave it alone to do its thing. It will only take a few minutes to install. The program itself will be encrypted. If anyone ever tries to mess with it to figure it out it will delete itself, if it can't stop them. This program will be how we will communicate from now on and it also will be my gift to the Knight family and all of our brothers and sisters and whoever we trust enough in the media.

"Oh, and get rid of this as soon as you've read it. Now, there are features that you don't have to worry about. When you need to talk and it doesn't matter who reads in, just type and I'll get your message. If you need to discuss something that you don't want anyone else to see, there is a dot the size of a nickel in the exact center of the screen. The dot is not visible, but the screen will flicker twice very quickly when your cursor is on it. Click that spot. This will take you to the backside of the program. Type in the password, and then we can chat without prying eyes. All of our discussions there are encrypted and private. If anyone tries to mess with it, it sends out a virus from hell that will shut their computers down." Jonathan spent the next few months setting up other Knight members remotely and fixing any bugs. They tested and retested the program until it worked flawlessly.

The President called for calm and people began settling down after not knowing if this was a onetime occurrence or if the planes destroying the Trade Centers were just the beginning. Jonathan was called up and sent to the Middle East to interrogate captured terrorists.

He tried as hard as he could to remember if any of them had been on those training fields on his mission to Sudan. Jonathan thought of how many deaths were allowed to occur because they were told to stand down and their reports had been unread and filed away. He thought maybe those people who died on 9/11 would still be alive had they taken down some of these young Jihadists back then. In his travels abroad, he stayed in touch with both his agency and with Peter, Azad, Fadil and other members of the Knight family. As promised, they shared information with one another. Had the CIA or Peter's agency known, they would have both been in serious trouble. Israel would not have come down so harshly on Azad and Fadil if they were caught.

Israel was ground zero for the terrorists' hatred and could use all of the help they could get. However, they were still unaware of Azad and Fadil's work with the Knights. Eventually, all four men found themselves in various countries in the Middle East working undercover, interrogating suspects and trying to prevent another major attack. Little by little they gathered information that began to paint a picture for them. Individually, the information that they gathered started to make sense. With the help of Azad, Fadil and other Arab members of the Knight family, they realized that this was not a culmination of hurt pride or acts of colonialism from some western nation; it was meant to destroy the U.S. economy and push for a war. Bin Laden was pushing the envelope; his hatred for the U.S. drove him to extreme measures and with the help of religious fanatics he could pull this off. They had underestimated his strength and determination. He had surrounded himself with willing fighters who had prepared and waited like a snake waits for its prey, striking at the right time.

It was a religious war that at first was hard for Jonathan and Peter to comprehend. This was a Holy War that to Arabs had been being waged since God had forsaken Ishmael, Abraham's first son with his wife's handmaiden, Hagar and Abraham gave favor instead to Isaac, Abraham's son by his wife, Sarah.

In their travels, they heard Arabs speak of this biblical slight by God against the descendants of

Ishmael as the reason for retribution against descendants of Isaac. Mohammed and the Koran in 600 AD didn't help matters. In fact, it gave verification and justification for hardline Arabs. It called for anyone that did not give in to Islam be subjugated or killed. It was that simple. Sure, there were other things that upset them but they just added fuel to a fire that had already been burning for centuries. Jonathan began to realize that Arabs were the most patient but least tolerant people he'd ever run across.

Little by little, the agents all began to see that leaders in these oil rich Middle Eastern nations were reinvesting in Western nations. Not as much for the financial investments but for their future desires to turn those nations into Islamic countries that were Sharia Law compliant. Christians had been given the same mission to spread the gospel, but somewhere along the way had become side-tracked and no longer took it as seriously as the Muslims were.

The agents discovered that Arabs were using their wealth from greedy western businessmen to buy off greedy Western politicians. Arabs saw the lack of passion from Western religious leaders and thought them to be weak and ineffective leaders of their churches who would rather sit on their laurels than die for their own salvation. Not only did Jonathan and Peter see and hear it from the people they met in their undercover travels in the Middle East, they began finding proof of it. It was becoming clear to them that underneath the surface rhetoric, Muslims were buying off Western politicians.

All during this time, Jonathan was experiencing an awakening. He wasn't sure at the time if it was a spiritual awakening or something else. He began to see the future of what his children would have to go through if he ever met the right woman and settled down. What kind of future would his children have in the United States if it was auctioned off to Islam or a communist country? Would his children have to live a life of fear of being in constant danger at the hands of a tyrannical government because of some politician's short-sighted greed? Not just his kids or his family but every family would have to live with the consequences.

It was thoughts like this that made Jonathan volunteer to serve his country from the beginning. It was thoughts like this that made him decide to move forward with plans. The good fortune to be a part of the Knight family with a seemingly unlimited amount of human and financial resources made him think he could pull it off. All aircraft travel was suspended for three days after the attacks. Jonathan heard little from his handlers at the CIA. They, like the rest of the country had been caught off guard. It had been arrogance that had put the country at risk. *How dare they attack us on our own soil, with our own airplanes despite the fact that he and other CIA agents had warned their superiors?* No one cared to listen. Now they were scrambling to cover their asses. Jonathan had been an agent long enough to know that the spin machine was busy at work. His bosses would be busy at work preparing for Congressional hearings instead of finally dealing with the problems at hand. As long as they put all the pieces in place and everything sounded right, no one would know the difference. They could always say that the information being sought was classified. Classified was short for ignored or thrown in a file somewhere and never read. Jonathan called a few of his colleagues from the agency to see what they had heard. Over the years, Jonathan learned of a few agents who were part of the Knight family. They had even called on him to help them on various assignments.

The spy business was a risky one. You could never be sure who was a mole for the agency. However, the Knights had a good reputation so far. No one had ever turned as far as he knew. Maybe they had been screened really well, maybe it was the freedom the Knight family gave its brothers and sisters once they became part of the organization, or maybe it was the credit card that each is given with unlimited funds that kept them loyal. After all, there are few organizations that give that kind of trust to an agent. By the powers to be within the family, an agent could be anywhere living like a king. At least until he was found. If he was ever found. No one had ever taken that chance. *Who knows*, he thought. The family may have just written it off and moved on.

Chapter Sixteen

It wasn't long before Jonathan was sent on various assignments by his agency, the CIA. It was time for him to cover some old ground and send them reports. As he sent them in, he found his bosses to be at least more attentive. There was a trip back to Sudan then on to Afghanistan, Saudi Arabia and Iraq to try to track down solid information on the terrorists. His bosses didn't know he was sharing that same information with those in the Knight family and they were sharing what they learned with him. At times, they would use his software to communicate. At other times they communicated by satellite phone. Nothing would be suspected by their speaking to each other by phone. If anyone back at the agency was listening they would not hear anything mentioned about the Knights in those conversations.

During the Christmas holiday in 2002, Jonathan found himself along the northern most border of Iraq making new friends with Kurdish rebels who were already preparing to fight against Saddam Hussein. Jonathan and several other men had been dropped into a zone that was already established as a safe zone. The area was mountainous and rugged and so were the Kurds that lived there. They were, however, friendly to anyone who wanted to bring down Saddam. Along with the agents, several pallets of money, weapons, ammunition, food and other supplies were also dropped. These supplies were to be used to soften Saddam's forces and keep them busy and distracted. The rebels did exactly that.

Jonathan really didn't see the necessity of it when the war started. There were days of bombing followed by troops coming in to sweep up the mess. Peter, Azad and Fadil found themselves in similar situations during the war. All were busy. They were taking it all in and looking for a way to make inroads against an enemy that didn't fight fair if there was such a thing in war—an enemy that went on the world's stage and screamed about injustice but didn't have any qualms hiding behind a school full of innocent women and children. An enemy that would use a shoulder-fired missile to bring down a commercial airliner filled with vacation travelers and then run back to the United Nations and complain about soldiers from Western nations killing a child unintentionally.

Those same Western nations were tied and bound by the Geneva Convention, the United Nations, the liberal media and a truckload of ACLU lawyers lived and enjoyed the privileges of freedom, but helped the enemy destroy it every chance they got. Jonathan knew that time had changed him since college. He knew that the world had changed as well. Terrorists made sure of that on 9/11 and he knew that he would never let it go. He saw too much suffering they had caused to advance their religious beliefs. All countries have conflicts with other nations during their existence. He knew that the United States had its share of them but still stood for freedom, not like those nations that didn't allow their citizens basic human rights and freedom of religion.

Jonathan knew that he'd eventually have to decide if the cross he was about to pick up was going to be something he could handle or was it too much for him to bear. He knew that he had reached a crossroads in his life, a point where he could not turn back. He knew that God was tugging on his heart and soul to do something. He was getting a message even though he didn't know yet what it was. God had given him of all people a unique opportunity to be a fountain instead of a drain and he knew that in the end he'd end up answering the call. Before he did though, he thought it was time to have a little fun after several years of nothing but work. His missions in Iraq and other assignments like tracking suspected terrorists as they traveled had helped him gain insight into what he knew he had to do.

It was 2009. Another president had been elected a year earlier. The Knight Family knew who he was but his rise to prominence happened fast. They had heard the chatter about this man, Franklin Corona. They knew he was nothing more than an international two-bit hustler that had the good fortune of being at the right place at the right time. He had the backing of those who realized his potential of being a facilitator to bring radical groups together. He was a sales person and an organizer. No one in the Knight Family believed he'd actually become President. They had given the American voting public too much credit. With the aid of the media, (who were for the most part Liberal Progressives), the public had been convinced that this person was the answer to all of their problems. The Knights were aware of the problem but couldn't stop a presidential election without drawing attention to themselves. The American people had elected a man who had no basis or love for the United States other than what it could offer him and give to his friends. Even before he was sworn in,

Jonathan put him on his watch list and informed the Knights of his plan that he would discuss with his core team when they met if they could all take a vacation. Jonathan had decided to take on an American president who was hell-bent on changing the country into a lesser power.

Heroes weren't born heroes; they usually found themselves in a situation that makes them either rise to the occasion or be swept away in the currents of history never to be seen or heard from again.

Chapter Seventeen

It was time for a break. Jonathan contacted his friends Peter, Azad and Fadil and asked them if they could hang out for a few weeks. They hadn't had a chance to meet for a little partying since their days in Amsterdam back in the 1990s, although they often spoke on the phone or chatted on the software Jonathan had developed. They spent short times working together on various projects in the Middle East while on assignments.

He worked with Azad in Israel in 2003, when a Hamas suicide bomber killed seventeen people and wounded fifty-three. He detonated a bomb hidden under his clothing in the Haifa bus 37 massacre. Jonathan was still in Israel when less than thirty days later, a Palestinian suicide bomber detonated a suicide vest and killed himself outside a crowded cafe in the Mediterranean coastal city of Netanya, wounding nearly forty people, two of them critically. In 2005, Jonathan was sent to work in England for several months to help investigate a suicide bombing attack on a double-decker bus and three London Underground trains, killing fifty-two people and injuring over 700. This happened, on the first day of the 31st G8 Conference. These attacks were the first suicide bombings in Western Europe.

Jonathan didn't work with Peter on the assignment but had a chance to meet with him and several other members of The Knight Klan on different occasions to socialize and share what they learned. Now, he hoped to have time to hang out with them, have some fun and discuss what needed to be done to help save the world. Jonathan posted a message on the Knight's bulletin board that he'd created asking Peter, Azad and Fadil if they could join him on vacation. They all made it a habit to check their bulletin board out regularly, and they all agreed that they deserved a vacation and Cyprus was a good choice. The nightlife and luxuries offered on the little island that sat below Turkey in the Mediterranean wasn't a place Jonathan or any of the other guys had been.

Now that the vacation was arranged and scheduled to happen in two weeks, Jonathan decided to visit his parents and sister for a few days beforehand. He called them, but had seen them only occasionally on holidays and even then he never stayed home much while he was there. He would check in at his parents' house, unpack and then go visit other friends and family. He promised himself that this time he'd actually spend some time with them, go to church and watch television with them. They were getting older and that was pretty much their life now. They spent years worrying about his safety. At Christmas, they didn't seem as worried about him and he wasn't really sure why.

His parents were religious and his mom had told him before that whenever he left after visiting that she turned him back over to God. When he got there, he did just as he had promised himself and stayed close to them. He wasn't sure at this point if he'd ever see them again. His dad asked what he was up to and Jonathan told him that the war had kept him busy with travel. His dad knew he couldn't give him many details and Jonathan knew that was what his dad wanted to hear. Jonathan really wanted to be able to share his stories and adventures with his dad and sometimes he just wanted to have his dad's advice like he did as a child. He wanted to go fishing or play a game of basketball with his dad out in the front yard, but he knew his dad wasn't physically capable anymore. He wanted his mom's cooking. That he got plenty of while he was home.

He helped his dad around the house and out in the yard and they talked. Jonathan did tell him some things, but didn't want to ever give too much information and put his parents' lives at risk. Neither knew much about his life as a spy. He had always just told them he was an officer on "special assignments". His dad as former military knew what that meant and knew that few of his questions would ever be answered about his son's job again. "Mom, I'm going on vacation to Cyprus next week with some friends. On the way back, I'm going to stop by Germany and see Grandma and some of the cousins. What do you want me to bring you back from there?" he asked. She replied, "Bring your mother back a wife for you and some grandchildren. That's all your dad and I want to see one of these days."

Her comments didn't surprise him. She always bugged him about settling down and having kids. "Okay Ma, I will but what if she's a mermaid? I don't think people can have kids with mermaids." She just smiled at him. She knew that she would get a smart aleck answer from him. She knew her Jonathan. "Hey, look Ma, I really haven't met anyone special yet." She replied, "You've got all of these good looks. Who are you wasting it on? You're not gay are you?" Nothing she said shocked him; his sister had the same attitude as his mom. A person would never know what would come out of their mouths. Jonathan loved it, although he was more of a quiet type like his dad. The time arrived for him to leave for Cyprus. He had packed a couple of extra suitcases for his trip there and would leave these suitcases there at his parents' house. He knew he would have to stop back through after his trip to Cyprus and then to Germany. His grandma would have some things for his mother—spices, coffee, and chocolate that his mom couldn't find in the U.S. The morning of his departure for Cyprus, he gave both parents a big and long hug.

He kissed his mom on the cheek and shook his father's hand. His father gently gripped Jonathan's hand and said, "Son, I know what you do, you know that. I just want to say I'm proud of what you're doing, thank you and you know I love you. There are not very many people who can or do what you do. You've sacrificed a lot along the way to help keep me, your mom, sister and everybody else safe and free. I know something's afoot and I know you won't and can't tell me about it, but whatever it is...you be careful. I'm an old man now, but if you're ever any trouble, call me. I'll find a way to help you if it's the last thing I do here on this earth." Jonathan choked back the tears that were welling up in his eyes and said, "I know you will Dad and you and Mom do the same, okay. I gave sis my satellite phone number and another way to reach me if there's a problem." Just as he was finishing his comment, a horn was blowing out front. "It's my cab Dad. I'll be in touch with you. Take care of Ma like always."

With that, Jonathan went to his bedroom and grabbed his suitcases and hugged them again before walking outside to the taxi that would take him to the airport. Jonathan arrived at the airport and checked his baggage. He had decided to fly first class for a change. He had only sparingly used the card given to him by the Knights and had never used his Jonathan Knight identity. On this trip he was Jonathan Knight. There was some fun to be had and a job to do. Jonathan's four-hour flight from San Antonio to Atlanta was uneventful. On the first leg of the trip he flew coach. In Atlanta he had a short layover, so he checked out the bar and had a drink. The television above the bar was tuned to the news.

He couldn't hear over the muffled conversations in the bar, but he could see that the President was on and giving a speech. At first he started to move over closer to be able to hear, but he decided against it. He was officially on vacation and didn't feel like upsetting himself so he decided to just people watch those in the bar and the people that could be seen walking through the terminal through the plate glass window. Soon enough, he was being called to board his plane to Cyprus. Jonathan got on, settled into his seat and ordered a drink. Before today he hadn't had a drink in sometime so he ordered a Dirty Martini.

Chapter Eighteen

He noticed the flight attendant had been a little overly friendly while taking his order. It made him think, had other women flirted with him over the past few years and he just not noticed or was he doing something different today. Jonathan's good looks and athletic build had always attracted women, but his mind was always somewhere else. Lately it has been on the horrors of war. *Not this trip* he thought. The flight attendant returned with his drink and he said, "Oh, I forgot to tell you...shaken, not stirred." She smiled. Not everyone knew the line from the James Bond movies. She did and asked, "So, you're a spy. Can I get you anything else, Mr. Bond?" Jonathan returned the quip, "We can start with your phone number. I know you're working, but it would be really nice to get to know you if you have time to talk with me." "I think I can manage that. There aren't many passengers today."

She turned and walked towards the back of the plane. Jonathan turned around in his seat to watch her walk away. As she reached the curtain separating first class from coach, she turned and looked at Jonathan and smiled again before disappearing behind the curtain. Her name was Kathlen. At the galley she could hardly concentrate on her drink order from another passenger. She met hundreds of men on her job and none had shaken her like this one. Kathlen could have been a model. She had received several offers but she turned them down. She ran track on scholarship at the University of Oklahoma and earned a degree there in Divinity.

She planned on being the first female pastor at her church back in her hometown in Georgia. Her plans changed after her marriage of less than two years fell apart. She had married her college sweetheart who played basketball at the University of Oklahoma. He started off as the type of guy that she always wanted. He planned to go to medical school after graduating but never made it. After their wedding they moved back to Georgie and rented a townhouse in Atlanta. She quickly landed a job as a Youth Pastor there and he continued his studies on scholarship. She knew that eventually she'd have to get used to his being gone for long hours. She just didn't know it would be so soon. After months of him not explaining why he was coming home so late, she eventually found that he was cheating on her.

So much for marriage, she thought as she finished mixing the drink. It'd been over a year since her sudden divorce. She had lost faith in humanity so she decided to get away and travel as a flight attendant. She had no interest in men until now. Kathlen took the drink back to the passenger who was a few rows ahead of Jonathan. As she was passing him, she glanced over and he was busy typing something on his laptop. After delivering the drink, she stopped next to Jonathan and asked him, "Are you ready for another drink sir?" Jonathan looked up from his computer and smiled at her and said, "No, thanks. That was my second drink in about five years. I'd better pace myself."

She nodded and asked if she had interrupted him. He replied, "Not really, I was just sending a message to the friends I'm meeting in Cyprus. I just told them that I just met my future wife and to make sure to set some time aside for our wedding." Kathlen laughed, "Wow, you've got it all planned huh? You don't even know my name yet." "Hi, I'm sorry. My name is Jonathan." She extended her hand, "I'm Kathlen. Well Jonathan, I'm going to stop back by to talk, but I can't sit down." "I understand. I'll be here," he said. Kathlen stopped for periods during the eight-hour flight to talk to Jonathan. Jonathan would have a two- hour layover in Frankfurt and Kathleen had two days off. They agreed to meet for coffee in the airport Starbucks after landing. At the airport, Jonathan, using his new identity, had to go through customs. Kathlen told him it would be about fifteen to twenty minutes before was getting off the plane after landing, but they arrived at the coffee shop within minutes of each other.

They ordered coffee, sat down and began talking. "Well, Mr. Bond, what do you do?" Jonathan paused for a moment and said, "I'm in the military. I'm a computer programmer." She thought for a moment, "So, you are a spy?" she asked. "Not really, I look for terrorist traffic on the computer. It's like playing video games all day." She asked another question, "Do you know anyone in Cyprus? Is there a long lost girlfriend there?" He knew she was hinting, giving him a chance to come clean if he was involved with someone. He answered. "No, there is no girlfriend, never been married and no children." She wasn't done with the interrogation. Jonathan found himself on the other side of the table for change. She continued before Jonathan could have a turn. "So you're one of those eternal bachelors." Jonathan found an opening, "Not at all, it's just a vacation. I'm meeting some male friends there and we're just going to play golf. You know, do fun stuff for guys. I haven't been on a vacation for a really long time."

They continued to engage in small talk until it was time for Jonathan to leave. He promised to call her when he was back in the States. Kathlen knew that she'd be looking forward to the call. They hugged goodbye and parted. Jonathan headed to board his plane for the hour and a half trip to Cyprus.

Chapter Nineteen

Jonathan got there just shy of 3:00 pm. Peter, Azad and Fadil picked him up in a four-door BMW. As Jonathan threw his luggage into the trunk, he shouted to Azad who was still behind the wheel. "Do you have a hook up on cars here too?" Azad smiled and shot back, "How did you know Jonathan? Doesn't hurt to have friends. This person doesn't own a dealership. He just has more cars than he can use at one time." As Jonathan got in, everyone happily greeted him, slapping him on the back and high-fiving each other. If anyone had seen them, they were just a group of ex-college students reuniting after years apart.

They wouldn't have been far off, but these men carried with them years of working among some of the most hardened and murderous human beings on the planet and had walked away alive each time. "We're starving Jonathan; we haven't eaten since we got in this morning." "No problem, you guys go ahead. Stop and get something. I'm not hungry." They all started teasing him about his new love interest. "Love does that to a person," Azad quipped. Peter added to the teasing, "When's the big day pal?" Jonathon shook his head. "Not soon. I'll send you guys an invite. You'll all be in the wedding party."

Azad pulled into the parking lot of a restaurant. "What do they have here?" Fadil asked. "Who knows? You've eaten Camel Spider before. What do you care?" Azad shot at him. "Yes, but she tasted much better than your mother," Fadil joked. The men piled into a booth inside the restaurant. They were back among friends.

Fadil told them that he couldn't stay with them for the whole two months because of his wife back home. "Wife?" Peter asked. "Yeah, what wife?" Jonathan asked. Fadil didn't talk much about anything usually, so in reality he just never spoke of her which wasn't unusual for an Arab man. It was pretty obvious that Azad and Peter weren't married, if they were then Jonathan figured he'd really be in for a shock. Peter had two children back in England from a previous marriage. He was married right after he joined the military. He tried to make it work but the strain of the job was too much for the both of them. They left on good terms, though. His wife, Diane never remarried so Peter had a chance to drop in when he wasn't working. "Hey Pete. How are the kids?" Jonathan asked, changing the subject away from himself to a more serious discussion. "Oh, they're great, Jon. Thanks for asking. Little Shelly's five now and Johnny's three. They're quite a handful for Diane. I just left them; they're all doing great. The children said to tell Uncle Jon hello. Diane sends regards as well." The guys wrapped up eating in short order, paid and went back to the car. The hotel Azad drove up to looked fabulous. The guys had told him about it, but he recognized that their descriptions had been understated when he walked into the lobby. "Jonathan, we know you probably have jet-lag. Not sure if you want to head up to your room or grab a massage right down the hall. That was the first thing we did this morning after getting here," Peter said. "I think I'm going to go up to the room and catch you guys when I wake up," Azad said. "You should find everything you need. Call us later. We'll leave a message on your phone with our suite numbers. We also will be in our rooms. I think I'll spend some time on Facebook."

They all parted and went to their rooms. Old friends reunited, it felt good to be among friends so they could be themselves and not have to worry about every word being said. Jonathan went to his room and straight into bed. Within a short time he was asleep. Peter entered his room and turned on the television. It had been a while since he watched a game of soccer. So he searched until he found one. With a moment of quiet time, Fadil called home.

After telling his wife that he was okay and all of his friends were now together at the hotel, he asked how the kids were doing and told her he'd be home in a few weeks. They talked for a few more minutes and then after hanging up, Fadil lay on the bed and enjoyed the quiet.

Azad pulled his laptop out of the bag. His room had Wi-Fi and as he was only going to be on Facebook he didn't worry too much about using his own connections to login securely.

He had several thousand Facebook friends who he'd sometimes chat with knowing that he'd probably never meet any of them. However, they helped him keep up with the politics of mainly the United States in real time, and gave him a sense of the mood of the people there. He realized how important the happenings in the United States affected the wellbeing of Israel and the world. There was one blogger in particular whose writings he followed. She was an American who wrote mainly about politics, but it seemed that whatever came to her mind at the moment would be a topic of discussion for her and her thousands of online friends, even though the majority of her subject material showed her to be conservative and very patriotic towards her country. He clicked on to her link and went into her site.

He was curious what she'd written today. It might also give rise to questions that Jonathan would be able to answer and explain to him while they were there. He thought back to Jonathan's message about moving forward with a plan of attack of his own. Had he dropped it? All of them had been so busy prosecuting the war on terror that they couldn't do much to help the Knight family wage its own war on terror besides providing them with information. Azad had a feeling that was about to change for them. Fadil had been tracking some of the members of the Royal Saudi family. So had he. They both knew that Prince Mussab would also be in Cyprus during the time that they were there. The Prince had bought a new yacht and had wanted to take it out. He would inform Jonathan and Peter of the Prince's movements and hopefully, they'd be able to get close enough to him and learn some things about what was going on inside Saudi Arabia. With any luck, they would also be able to compromise at least one person that was a staffer aboard the Prince's yacht or maybe the Prince himself.

Azad reigned in his thoughts long enough to glance at Julie's blog post. It was an article about Religion this time. She was complaining about the persecution of Christians who ventured into Muslim or Communist lands and tried to do missionary work. She had written the article with such urgency and compassion that it was if she had suffered under persecution herself or channeled one of the victims with whom Azad dealt. Some he had been able to rescue but most he had not. Many were still out there, either captives in their own homes or in a prison or jail cell somewhere waiting on the next beating or death.

Azad brought himself out of his daydream. He was on vacation but it would be hard to leave his work behind after so many years of seeing the underbelly of life and the cruel nature and contempt that the corrupt, greedy people of the world had for their fellow man. Azad closed the cover on his laptop and lay on the bed. He would have to try to enjoy this vacation. He had a feeling that he and his three friends were going to need clear heads and energy for what they were about to undertake. He wasn't sure exactly what it was yet, but God was telling him to prepare. The sun was setting and Jonathan was awake. He rolled over and saw that he had missed a call. He called the front desk. It had to be one of the guys calling to see if he was up. It was Peter. He had asked what was up for the evening. Jonathan was still groggy.

Chapter Twenty

Jonathan called Peter and told him that he preferred just to have dinner with them and hang out on the beach. He wanted to go over some of his ideas and was ready to get going even though he planned on relaxing and enjoying himself. Peter as usual was easy. Jonathan called Fadil and Azad. They'd meet out by the pool within the hour and then go find a secluded spot to talk. As agreed, they met at the pool that had a spectacular ocean view. Even though the sun was setting, the weather was warm and perfect for swimming. The men walked up the beach a ways and found a small lighted pavilion with wooden tables and attached bench seats. The Mediterranean breezes wafted through the covered shelter. There was no one there except a waitress standing near the bar. She saw them coming in and walked over to take their drink order.

Azad looked the waitress over from head to toe and then over again. He thought to himself for a moment before deciding the girl looked too young for anything permanent. She was a native and she looked to be in her early twenties. She must have been a mind reader because before walking away she did the same to Azad. After her apparent approval she smiled at him and walked away. She brought back their drinks and sat each one in front of each person. She looked up and gave them the price. Azad looked for and found his Knights card and paid her. The tip must have surprised her. She again smiled at Azad and said in English that she'd bring his receipt and card back after processing it at the bar. She came back and Azad signed the receipt and gave it back to her along with a note introducing himself and his hotel room number. She left the receipt on the tray and put the note in the pocket of her tight form fitting jean shorts.

Peter's speaking awakened Azad from his trance as he watched the girl's round hips float away from the table and back to her station near the bar. "Azad, are you still with us or are you somewhere else? If so, can you tell us about it? It might be worth paying to hear." Azad grinned sheepishly, "I'm here Peter but as a spy, I just had to make sure we were all safe. You never know these days." The men all laughed. Jonathan moved closer in to be heard even though they were alone. "Look guys, we've been chasing our tails for a really long time. Something needs to be done. We seem to be losing ground." They all nodded in agreement. Fadil asked him, "What did you have in mind Jonathan? I totally agree with you."

Jonathan knew they would ask him this question. It was an age old question. "Our governments think this Muslim problem is our fault and they're upset with our behavior over the years. I don't think it is. The countries that hate us and kill us at every opportunity sure have no problem taking our money. Then they use it against us. Our citizens are at war with each other. Just as in each of our countries, you have the conservatives and the liberals. It seems that the conservatives have a better grip on the truth, especially since we got this new President." Peter was facing a similar situation in England. Perhaps even greater. The liberals there had allowed Arabs to gain even more ground and nearly dominate the nation and bring in Sharia law as a separate law. Little by little they had softened up judges and politicians to convince them that Sharia law would just be for Muslims in England. They also implemented some banking laws in the U.S. with the same excuse. This is against the U.S. Constitution where everybody is treated equally, but somehow they convinced government officials and even judges to make exceptions for the Muslim faith.

It was a tactic that they were using to populate, and then dominate a nation. They would now shut down traffic whenever something bothered them. They would bring out their prayer rugs and pray in the middle of the streets. It at first seemed cruel to arrest a man while he was praying, but their tactics had worked quite effectively as the average Britain cursed the inconvenience but did little to stop it. Peter commented, "Jonathan, they seem to be making terrible headway with decision makers. The powers that be make excuses for them. It's as if the Arabs have them in their pockets." Azad, now over the fantasy he was hoping to play out later, added, "Your leaders are in their pockets. We have tons of information on it. We thought you did too. Doesn't the CIA keep such information? We've been on this trail since shortly after we left Sudan. We've been tracking a number of leaders in many countries. Yours too Peter."

Jonathan and Peter looked at each other. They should not have been surprised by this revelation but as good agents they had followed instructions for the most part. They were supposed to investigate the bad guys. In their minds the bad guys always came from the other direction. It was becoming more and more apparent over the years, especially with the new President that the bad guys had found the key to the front door that was hiding under the mat. Now they had gone in the house and helped themselves to a sandwich, taken their shoes off and ordered a porn movie. Azad went on to say, "I can get you copies of my reports. Another thing. We have to keep an eye on Saudi Arabia. They are throwing a lot of money around. All over the Western World. They aren't doing it just to be nice.

Not just western leaders are on the take, church leaders are too. They make deals to look the other way when their missionaries are captured and tortured—or worse."

"What do you mean by church leaders? Are you saying that they get paid?" Jonathan asked in disbelief. "No, Jonathan. They look the other way. The churches pay them in this case. Not so much Saudi Arabia in this instance. They are not tolerant to any other religion being there. It's mostly other countries in the Middle East and Communist countries in Asian and Eastern Bloc countries. Major atrocities against Christians occur there and instead of the Western churches raising hell, nothing is said. They look the other way. These people are out there on a limb like sitting ducks." Peter couldn't resist Azad's odd choice of combining two English sayings so he joked, "Azad, you won't find too many ducks out on a limb. Too heavy."

Azad kept going, all but ignoring Peter's teasing, "You know what I mean, Peter. Seriously. These two things are big problems. If something needs to be done to help, we're going to have to get to the root of the problems." Fadil had been quiet, but joined in. "My take on the whole thing is this—this world is quickly going to hell if we don't do something. I mean, I'm away from my family, not just now but a lot of times doing my job to help protect my children's future. That's why I'm here. I see our being able to really help as part of the Knight family. They ask nothing of us except to help, when we want and how we want. We've all been busting our asses and getting nowhere for many years now.

Israel has the closest agency to compare to the Knight family because we have to. It's a matter of life and death for us. It's not just to move our interests forward; it's to survive. We are the nation for others to kick at every chance. I'm tired of it. Before I forget...I've been tracking a Saudi Prince his name is Adan Mussab. That is another reason I'm here Jonathan. At first when you said Cyprus, I thought you were too. Are you?" This was the first Jonathan had heard anything about a Saudi Prince being in Cyprus, so he asked, "What do you hope to learn?" Fadil answered, "I'm not sure. I'm just hoping that we can find him and make friends with him. It shouldn't be too hard to find a billionaire on a yacht on such a small island." Jonathan had asked for this. He shouldn't have expected anything but honesty from his friends and he was getting it. He processed what Azad and Fadil said and asked, "You guys have this information and it's all laid out there on the table for you, I mean, why me? Why Peter? There are other Knights with whom you could be working this. I know Peter and I are your friends, but really, why us? We could just come here, chill, have a good time and go home. I mean, I'm not even sure why I said Cyprus instead of Jamaica or somewhere. It could have been anywhere. Why did God direct me to pick Cyprus and then it just so happens that this Prince is here?" Peter spoke, "If I may. Jonathan I can't speak for Azad and Fadil, but I think I can answer your questions. There is such a thing as divine intervention. You...we, we're a part of that. I noticed it from the beginning. Your software for instance. What guided you to write it and then just give it away?"

Jonathan wasn't sure exactly where Peter was going with his question, but he answered. "I wanted to give something back. If it was something that was going to help...help the Knights. Help you guys...help our countries. Save the world, I don't know. Why?" Peter continued. "Has it helped?" Another question. "Not really. I mean I did it after 9/11. I had been working on it awhile, but finished up right after. We really haven't done much with it." Peter was slowly getting around to a point. "Because we need it now. We need it in God's time. There have been some things about you and all of us, but especially you that make me think that you have some kind of instinct about things. And I'm not saying that you always get it right. None of us do, but you get lucky with having things prepared—just too much to be luck."

Azad jumped in. "I'll give you an example. There is a lady on Facebook that I follow. She has that same insight. Fadil, Peter and I may find out things. That's our job, but you see the big picture. Her name is Julie. She reminds me of you. She does the same thing. She can see things like complex issues and break them down into pieces where others can easily understand them. This Prince thing. We know he will be here. That's it. We have other information as well. We all do. You are like a central processor on a mainframe computer. We can plug the information into you and you spit out the big picture. This lady Julie does the same thing. Some people have different gifts, Jonathan. God gives us what we can handle. When you spit out the information, it's not only the big picture...it's the right thing to do to help so many. Over the years in working with you, we've all noticed this gift that you have and we've discussed it. It's not luck Jonathan, it's your gift." Jonathan nodded. He didn't really understand fully what they were trying to tell him.

Chapter Twenty-One

"Who's this Julie person?" He thought that maybe by reading what Azad was talking about, he would understand what they were saying. Big picture guy? Azad said, "Okay, let's wrap it up here and go back to my room. She's on my laptop. I'll let you read her articles. Maybe then you'll understand." Back in Azad's room, he opened his laptop and once again signed on. He pulled up Julie's page, minimized it and then opened her blog. He then reopened the Facebook page. "Okay, start here. It's the article on religion. Then just scroll around and read. Do me a favor. Pray for God to open your eyes first." Jonathan smiled. "Are you serious?" He asked. Azad motioned to Jonathan as if he was about to whisper a secret to him and then said loudly, "Yes, I'm serious. We'll be in the living room. You stay here in the study for as long as you want. As long as God tells you to read...read."

With that, Azad, Fadil and Peter retreated to the living room to watch television and horse around like teenagers. Jonathan was starting to feel set up by his friends. He thought if they wanted him to lead the mission why they couldn't just ask instead of sending him back to school to read some blogger's article. He decided to play along, let them have their fun and give them a good laugh. Jonathan was only into the third paragraph of Julie's article when he became immersed in the story. Julie's style of writing put the reader into the same state of mind as of having a dream.

Jonathan was no longer reading. He was floating above a person being stoned in the Middle East for possessing a Bible. At first he was observing and then half of his body was buried in the sand. Before burying him, they had tied his hands behind his back and put a hood over his head. He knew he was about to die and he knew how. He saw darkness and tasted the sweat from his brows. He was thirsty as he prepared for the first and last instance of his head being crushed by stones. The first stone would make him see stars and his ears ring before the second and third hit their mark and ended his life there, somewhere in a hole in the desert. The article ended and Jonathan once again realized that he was alive and sitting in a hotel room.

His friends were in the next room and he was a CIA agent, not a Christian that just died in the desert. Where was he when this poor soul's life came to an end? Jonathan saw why the guys in the other room admired her work. Her article had not only made him think about this poor guy's plight, it made him ask himself why he and no one else heard of this death until now. Did Julie truly know of this happening, or was she writing this to make a stark point and raise awareness? *My God*, he thought. I'm in the CIA. I'm supposed to save people like this. That's why I joined. But he didn't. He didn't know. He just didn't know. What was this big picture they talked about? He lay back on the sofa. He wanted to read a few more articles and see if this one had been luck, but he laid back and let his thoughts be in control for a moment. He wasn't a writer who could draw somebody into a story. He wasn't much of a writer at all. He could write a good report, but not tell a story in such a way. As he sat there, he thought about the things Azad had just told him about Julie.

He read another of Julie's articles; the article was great just as they described. His thoughts moved to the Prince, to persecutions, to corruption to the solution. The bell rang. He was a child, running out of class and anticipating being free from school for the rest of the day. He ran to the car, knowing his father would be inside with a big smile waiting for him. From school, he'd either be going to karate lessons or soccer practice where his dad coached his team. His dad was always involved with his team somehow. He'd either be coach, assistant coach or bring the juice for the whole team. After practice, he'd go home to have the smell of something his mom was cooking greet him at the front door. After dinner he'd do homework, and then talk to his parents a little more or his parents would play a game with him and his little sister. He caught himself daydreaming again. What did this daydream have to do with the solution?

He realized that if the solution didn't work, he'd never have the chance to coach his child's soccer or karate lessons. If the solution was wrong and if he did have children, they might be living in a Western nation that had adapted a way of life to which he was unaccustomed and wouldn't want for his children. He understood why Peter, Azad and Fadil expected him to process the information on this mission and spit out the big picture. The picture was clear. He would be their Central Processor. He knew his role and recognized his gift. He thought for a moment more about how lucky and blessed he was to have friends like these who not only recognized his gift but helped him find it. How many people went their whole lives and never found their gifts? His mission was clear; it was to make sure children had the freedom to keep looking for their own gifts.

Maybe, just maybe they would have friends like his to help them.

He walked into the room where Peter, Fadil and Azad were watching a soccer match. "Who's playing?" he asked. "England's playing Germany, buddy. Germany's one point ahead, but the game just started. England's going to teach you guys what we're made of." Jonathan smiled, "No way Peter. You should know better than that. Why have you guys been holding out on me about this Julie person? She's fantastic. I wonder if she has an inside source." Azad looked away from the television towards him. "She's great. She's very popular. Who knows? She's got a lot of fans worldwide. She may have a source feeding her. She's got a couple of other writers with her and they're good, but she's better. I guess that's why she's the boss."

Jonathan continued, "I think we're going to need someone like her for what we're about to do. I'm going to need to talk to you guys. Pick your brains. I need to know as much as you know. We've ten plus years to cover. We know Daniel Pearl was killed by Khalid Sheikh Mohammed, we've had reporters raped and at least one that was raped and killed, Christians persecuted, Anwar al-Alwaki responsible for the recent attack killing our soldiers in Killeen.

We've been working on the fringes; killing off one egg as hundreds more are being hatched. We need to work both. Bottom up and top down. We also need to establish a trail for the money. Who's getting it? You guys said we've got leaders on the take and churches looking at future profits, so we can start there. Let's track the money first. Let's go find that Prince." Azad handed Jonathan a beer and they all finished watching the game. When Jonathan got back to his room later that night, he signed on, logged into a secure connection and opened up Julie's blog. He began reading one of Julie's dreams of being swept away in a crowd of Muslims in the United States. Sharia Law had been implemented and Julie had gone shopping without an escort. The religious police had spotted her. She had just witnessed a public beheading and she was afraid that she'd be next. As they grabbed her, she woke to find that it was only a dream. Was her dream a warning of things to come? It was ironic. Jonathan and his friends had just vowed that they would use their abilities and vast resources provided to them by the Knight family to never let that happen. He knew that the problem was much larger than he and the three men could handle on their own. He knew that he would need someone with a worldwide audience like Julie's and he knew the mainstream media could not be trusted to help them. It was then that he knew that he'd have to contact her and ask her to help. It was going to possibly put her in danger, but with the types of articles she was already writing on a daily basis it shouldn't take much to get her on board. He was going to recruit her as an unofficial agent of the Knight family. When and if they found something, she'd have to get the word out as quickly as possible and with her strong following of devoted fans, she'd be the one to do it. Jonathan logged into his secure program and began typing Julie an email. When she opened the email, his program downloaded itself into her computer. He didn't plan on telling her it was there until the time was right. When it was, he would tell her how to log into it to speak to his team without worrying about prying eyes seeing what was being discussed. He went on to write, "Hello Julie. I'm a big fan of your work. In fact, many of my friends are. I was just told this afternoon what a great writer you are and I have to agree with them, you are. Your dream about Sharia Law being possible in the United States is probably truer than you realize. Don't worry. Just know that there are people out there who are working to prevent it. I'm one of them and there are others. In the next few days, I will send you some information that will be useful to your publication. I really doubt anyone else has access to these revelations. You will be the first. Afterwards, I'll see if you've found it useful and posted it. If so, I will be sending you more. One thing though, the powers that be won't really appreciate the whole world knowing what they're up to, so you may want to take some precautions and I believe we can help you with that if you find that you need it. Thanks for taking the time to read this."

Chapter Twenty-Two

Jonathan knocked on Peter's hotel room door. "You ready to go?" he asked. Peter nodded. Jonathan had spent the night before reading Julie's articles until he fell asleep. The next day had been relaxing. They hung out on the beach, hit the massage parlor and ate well. They planned a night on the town and the time had come. They walked down the hall to Fadil and Azad's rooms; both men were dressed and ready to go. "So, where are we going?" Peter asked the group. "Let's just cruise the island and see what is happening," said Azad. They went to the desk and ordered a limo. The limo pulled up and they got in and asked the driver about the town's best night clubs. After the driver gave him his opinion about the ones he was familiar with, Azad told him, "Great, let's just cruise by a few of them first and then we can decide which one." None of the four men spoke Greek or understood the street signs along the way. They would need to pay the driver to stay nearby, although they had found at the hotel that the majority of the staff understood and spoke English fluently, including intelligence officers, all of whom spoke several languages, none of them Greek. Most of the night clubs were along the highway, not far from either direction of their hotel. The St Raphael

Resort was very nice. The staff was great. Everyone so far had been very friendly on this small Island. It was truly Paradise and so far removed from their daily lives as spies. For the moment at least, they could forget about work. That changed when they approached the first night club they saw the Prince Fadil had mentioned on their first day here. He was getting out of the limo ahead of them. "That's him," Fadil exclaimed. "That's who?" Peter asked. "Prince Mussab, the guy I was telling you about. I told you he was on the Island." They agreed that they would find a way to casually meet him. If his driver was staying to wait for him, they would need to keep an eye on him as well. If he was a smoker, at some point, he'd have to get out of the car. Either way, he would get out and probably talk. They would have to find a way to meet the Prince. All exited the limo and got in line. The door fee was expensive, excluding everybody on the Island except the wealthiest. Celebrities and dignitaries from around the world were known to visit and play there when visiting Cyprus without the worries of fans asking for an autograph or pestering them in any way. Cameras weren't allowed and cell phones had to be checked at the door. The security both in and outside of the club was almost invisible, but the four men knew it was there. After all they were more or less in the same business. Many of their counterparts often worked security to moonlight or full-time after they retired. Clubs like this paid well. It wasn't quite as good as being a member of the Knight family, in fact nowhere close. Jonathan and the others were using their Knight cards more frequently now and each of them had an identity that wasn't their own while they were there. Jonathan was a little smitten with the flight attendant and had told her a little more than he should, but he had a good feeling about her. He felt that he could trust her, although one could never know for sure. The line moved rather quickly. They each paid and went inside. The music was deafening, but good. In the dark, smoke and disco light-filled environment, people seemed to be moving wildly, but still in slow motion. One flash of light and a person's arms were up and milliseconds later, the person had moved and their arms were somewhere else, giving the person watching this party the feel of being drunk without ever having taking the first drink. The club was alive and people were everywhere and the raw smell of hormones was pouring down the faces of people that just left the dance floor. Jonathan and his friends were standing near the bar. All four men were tall. Each was over six feet and muscular. Each got flirts and accidental but really intentional touches and stares from both women and men. Peter was the first to be dragged to the dance floor as Jonathan, Azad and Fadil stood by the end of the bar sipping their drinks. It wasn't long before everybody was on the dance floor trying to remember how to dance and let go and have a good time away from the pressures and problems associated with being a spy in a world that was trying to kill each other. With each drink and each dance, the problems of the world seemed to fade more in the distance and the most important thing in the world was dancing in front of them. Even Fadil, who was married, was having fun. Later that night when a young woman tried to take him outside to have sex with him on the beach, he politely declined and said he was waiting on someone. She stomped away in a huff that lasted just a few minutes. She met another guy on the way to the bathroom that was more than happy to oblige her requests.

The Prince seemed to be a shy man. His great wealth didn't mean much with others who were also from wealth. They may not have been billionaire status as he was, but some were and others here didn't really care how much money their moms and dads had as long as it never ran out for them. Prince Mussab was nothing special to look at. He was dressed very well. His two bodyguards wore black suits. He was dressed casually, but elegantly. His jewelry was obviously expensive. When Middle Eastern men in non-Islamic nations were on the prowl, they typically didn't wear the normal attire they wore back home. Many Western women were aware of their strict religious practices back home and their treatment of women. Many of these same women were overly fearful of being kidnapped by one of them and taken back to Saudi Arabia. Jonathan and Fadil had taken a break from dancing and sat at a table not far from the Prince's table intentionally where both could casually observe him. He had been observing them as well. He particularly noticed the amount of attention that they were getting from women as he was getting very little. The Prince did quite well with women on his own turf. Women who ran in his circles of influence were often all over him because of his wealth. But it was places like this that determined a man's worth in an animalistic sense. It was here on this prairie that determined who the Alpha male was and was not, a place where physical prowess and sexual attractiveness determined who ate and who starved. All of his wealth meant nothing here in this club on this night. Instinctively, he knew that to be anyone here he would have to be a leader of a pack of males who were Alphas before he would get the attention he craved. A man with all he wanted and desired had nothing here except an empty glass sitting on a napkin, so he beckoned for the waitress to bring him another round. When she arrived to take his order he told her to take over a bottle of their best champagne to the four men at the table nearby and another whiskey sour for himself, although back home, his religion forbade him from drinking. That law was hardly enforced on anyone in the royal family. Back home their laws were mostly "do as I say, not as I do" laws, although none in the Family drank in public where others beneath them could see what they did. Their servants sometimes leaked such information to the people, but who really cared about that. If someone got too vocal in their opposition to what a Royal was doing they were brought up on trumped- up charges and either severely beaten or put to death. Being beheaded was a neat way to silence those who disagreed. Jonathan and Fadil accepted their gift from him and then waved at him and gave him a thumbs-up for the gesture. They walked over to the Prince's table to thank him, walking past his guards, both fairly big and athletic fellows. One was an Arab and the other looked to be a mixture of black and something else. The other Arab and the white guy were back on the dance floor. Jonathan and Fadil winked at one another, not believing their luck. Jonathan had yet to realize the course of events that he was now experiencing were more divine intervention than luck, because this trip had already set him on a path that would have bigger consequences than he knew at the time. When they got to his table Jonathan said, "Thank you for the champagne. It's excellent; can we offer you a glass of it?" The Prince gestured for them to have a seat and said, "No, gentlemen that would ruin the taste of this beautiful whiskey sour I'm drinking. I hope I didn't do the same with what you were drinking." Jonathan continued, "No, not at all. We won't disturb you; we just wanted to come over and thank you and after you're done drinking here, please join us. We've met a lot of nice people and I'm sure they'd love to meet you as well." Now, it was the Prince's turn to thank lady luck. His gestured had worked. It was easier than he thought. He wouldn't rush to join them. He would lie in wait for the right time. He told them, "I'd be happy to join you shortly. So are you guys having a good time?" as if he hadn't noticed that they were. "Oh yes," said

Fadil. "There are beautiful ladies that just won't stop hitting on us. Luckily, none of the guys have yet. We don't swing that way." Peter and Fadil returned to their table. Azad and Peter were back and deeply involved in conversations with two of the women with whom they had been dancing. Shortly after Jonathan and Fadil returned, several other women came over and they all began introducing one another. The Prince also saw that it was time to make his move and went over to join the party. Jonathan introduced him to his new friends gathered around the table. The night was light and cheerful. The laughter and drinks flowed. Azad and Peter had invited their dance partners back to the hotel room and Jonathan and Fadil decided to call it a night. Azad's and Peter's friends would accompany them in the limo. The Prince invited them to attend a party with him on his yacht on Sunday night, which was two nights away; he gave them his card. They all said their goodbyes as the club was closing and all got in their respective cars. Jonathan and Fadil said goodnight to the others and went to their rooms.

Chapter Twenty-Three

Jonathan opened up his laptop and went to Julie's site and began to read. It was time to do some research on the others that she worked with and get some background on them. He stayed awake for several hours. He found that Julie had three other workers. Each would be useful at some point. All were good, decent people. He uploaded his software into their computers. It wouldn't activate until it was turned on and they were communicating with Julie. The only one that might know of its existence could be the guy named Christian. It appeared that he had worked in computer cyber intelligence with the military, which would be very useful to Jonathan's mission if he and Julie decided to play ball. However, he knew that the chances of Christian discovering his software were slim. He would have to look for it because it wouldn't show up as malicious software. It was merely going to stay dormant until it was needed. Had it been a malicious attack, Christian had the knowledge and experience to delete it or possibly track him down. He'd have to walk lightly with this team. They were smart and well connected.

Jonathan wrote his second message to Julie. It read, "Hello Julie, I'm writing again as promised. There are some people that I would like for you to check into.

Nothing too difficult. We'll start off slowly and work our way up. In fact, we're doing the same thing. The dream you had of Sharia Law coming to America is closer than you realize. We're working to stop it. You'll just have to trust us on that one. There are several known politicians and diplomats that are working with the Saudis to make it happen. Not just from the United States but other Western nations as well. So far, we've been able to track them to France, Germany, the United Kingdom and other places. There are also some very large churches that obviously aren't proponents of Sharia Law, but they are looking the other way as they feel that they have maxed out their membership in their respective countries as much as possible and are chomping at the bit for Middle Eastern and Communist nations to let them expand into theirs. I personally don't think they realize who they're dealing with. The people they are negotiating with don't always play fair." Jonathan went on to provide her with the names of those involved. "We don't have the whole picture yet, but we think the current U.S. President and his administration are involved as well. So do you; I've read some of your other articles. What you are about to do Julie isn't exactly safe, but it's important. If you run this series you're going to need to start being aware of your surroundings at all times. I don't want to be the cause of something happening to you. That's not my intention. However, as we both know, the media will not cover this story if it any way hurts their chosen POTUS. If you publish this story by Wednesday, I will give you instructions on another mode of communications that is more secure. Most of the information in my attachment is laid out for you. All you will need to do is personalize it a bit as you are so talented in doing." Jonathan attached the information that he had collected from his and his friend's databases and pressed "Send." All he could do now was to wait and pray.

Chapter Twenty-Four

The next morning Peter called Jonathan. "Hey bud. How was your night?" Jonathan asked. "Oh, fantastic thanks. I needed that. What about you? You had women hanging all over you. Why didn't you partake?" Peter asked. "I don't know. I wasn't feeling it. After all these years of being single and one-night stands with some beautiful women, I would have to meet someone I can't take my mind off of on the way here to Paradise," Jonathan responded. "I totally understand friend. I mean I would have expected Fadil to reel it in, but not Jonathan the Lady Slayer," Peter kidded. "Yeah, it was a bit out of character for me to just walk away from the candy jar like that but....anyway. I've got some news. That lady Julie. I've been in touch with her. I've sent her the second message. I did it last night. We should be okay. She can be very helpful if she plays ball. I also had a chance to research her staff. The only one we need to be concerned about is ...well, I forgot. We're not on a secure line. What's up for today?" Jonathan had abruptly changed the subject. "We were thinking about playing some golf. The weather's gorgeous. We can get a 10:00 am tee-time." That day on the golf course was spent planning for the next night. The Prince had given them an invitation to his yacht.

Jonathan called him and asked if it was still on. He told him they were all playing golf and apologized for not having thought to invite him but that it was a spontaneous event. On Sunday afternoon, they had a limo drive them to the harbor where the Prince's yacht was docked. There were already other guests arriving that the Prince might have invited from the night before. They boarded. The yacht was more of a mansion than a boat. The workmanship was exquisite. Everything was trimmed with wood and gold. The men had expected nothing less from their new friend. It was all paid for with the profits from oil. The Prince spotted them and quickly came over to greet them. "Gentlemen. Welcome. Make yourselves at home. The bar is over there and so is the food. I'll need to greet everyone, but I'll be back to check on you," he said and then left. It wasn't long before the yacht turned into a recreation of the club they had visited two nights before. They weren't sure if this would be the place to befriend and compromise him. For now, they would just enjoy themselves and let him make the first move. There had to be a reason he invited them. They would just have to sit back and wait to see what it was; they couldn't afford to be too aggressive. They had been right. The opportunity never came that night. The scene was too wild and loud. The Prince was flittering around and flirting. They would need to invite him to something and get him into their own arena. Something more quiet. As they were preparing to leave, they flagged him down and told him they had a great time and they would have to return the favor. He accepted. They would call him later and arrange something. They left and went back to the hotel.

Chapter Twenty-Five

The next day, Jonathan called the Prince and thanked him again. It was early afternoon and it seemed as though Jonathan had woken him. "Hey, Jonathan," Prince Mussab exclaimed as if he had known Jonathan for years. "I was going to call you guys." "Did I wake you?" Jonathan asked. "No worries. What's up for tonight?" That question came sooner than Jonathan expected. Jonathan didn't let on. "We don't have any plans for now. Why don't you stop by the hotel later tonight? We can meet at the bar and then decide where we all go from there. You don't have a curfew, do you?" Jonathan teased. "Hell no man. No chains around my neck. "Where are you guys staying?" Jonathan gave him the name and address of the hotel. After hanging up, Jonathan called his friends to let them know about the call. They were ecstatic. The hotel bar was the perfect place to meet him. The bar would be quiet. It was a Wednesday. At about 8:30 that evening, the Prince walked in alone without his bodyguards. He looked around for a minute before his eyes adjusted to the low light. He spotted his new friends sitting in the corner. Jonathan, Peter, Azad and Fadil all heartily welcomed him as if they were old friends. "Hey buddy, when can I borrow the yacht?" Azad asked him. "You know how to drive it?" Mussab jokingly replied. They laughed and started ordering drinks. Their conversation was about travel, women, family and sports. They were surprised at how much Mussab knew about American sports. Another thing that surprised them was that the Prince wasn't too happy when talking about his family and Saudi Arabia in general. Jonathan immediately picked up on it. He instantly thought back to the time he spent with his college professor, how she had discussed her father's decision to leave Saudi Arabia and how she had died on 9/11. "You have everything," Jonathan said to him. Prince Mussab said to him, "It's not about money, Jonathan. It's about how other people live. I've always lived a life of privilege but there is nothing special about me. Everyone deserves the right to become their own person. This is something to which a person aspires, not born into." Jonathan agreed with him. He knew the liquor wasn't the main reason Mussab was opening up to them. The liquor was only a lubricant that was helping it come out. Fadil spoke, "Mr. Mussab," "No, no. Call me Adan," the Prince said. "Okay Adan," Fadil continued. "Azad and I are both Arabs but we were raised in Israel. Why do your people continue to hate us? We are just a small country that wants to live in peace."

"You're right about my country Fadil. The majority of people do hate you. They believe and have been taught to believe that you should not exist. I of course am not one of them. People get along for the most part if the governments stay out of the way. In my country, my family is one of these governments. It is tradition but not all of us feel this way. We want to change or let me say, there are a few of us that want to see change. We travel the world because of our wealth. We go to the best universities and we meet people who are unlike us. People like you guys here. People that become friends and with whom we have no problems. My prayer is to live long enough to see this change. In defense of Saudi Arabia, your governments are not innocent in this matter. Truthfully, our wealth has allowed us to buy many Western leaders. In fact, soon..." his voice trailed off and he didn't finish his sentence. In an unexpected moment, Jonathan, Peter, Azad and Fadil knew they had their man. Prince Mussab would be their key to getting into Saudi Arabia. Peter saw that Jonathan was about to push the Prince and tapped Jonathan on the leg. Jonathan thought for a second. Peter was right. Now was not the time. Instead he said, "Okay, who wants to go party?" Prince Mussab held up his empty glass, "If you guys don't mind, I'm having a great time here just talking to friends. When a man is wealthy, women come and go. Good friends are rare." Peter ordered another round. "Seriously," the Prince continued. "I'm ready to settle down. What about you guys?" Peter responded, "I'll be ready in a few years. I'm waiting on Ms. Right but keep meeting Ms. Right Now." Azad quipped, "No way, not yet. I'm having too much fun."

What about you Jonathan?" the Prince asked. The others looked at Jonathan and started giggling. Well, I met someone flying over."

"We must celebrate, bring her over." the Prince said. "Let's have a party on my yacht." Jonathan instinctively saw an opening.

"We'll probably have to disinfect it and call in an exorcist first," Azad joked. "You know Prince, I have someone I want you to meet. She's from Italy, very beautiful. She reminds me of a young Sophia Loren. She's smart, she's an art dealer. Very smart, very classy. Want to meet her?"

What about your friends here?" the Prince asked.

"Don't worry. Fadil has to get home to the wife tomorrow. Peter and Azad will scrounge something up. I'll call Gina see if she is free to come down to meet you and ask if Kathlen, the girl I met, can join us for the weekend." Peter, Azad and Fadil quickly caught on to what Jonathan was doing. Jonathan had intentionally slowed down on his drinking. By the end of the night, he had only downed a couple of dry martinis. Fadil was the only one in the group that wasn't drinking alcohol. He never did. Prince Mussab, Peter and Azad were matching each other drink for drink. For a religion where drinking was forbidden for the most part, the Prince was not the typical Muslim, it seemed.

Chapter Twenty-Six

Jonathan sent a note to Julie asking that she forward anything she had coming out of Saudi Arabia to him. He also sent out a bulletin to the Knights asking for the same thing. Jonathan then walked down the hall and knocked on Fadil's door. He could hear the TV still on. "Yes," Fadil said. "It's me, Jonathan." Fadil opened the door and invited him in. Jonathan sat on the sofa and Fadil lay back on the bed. "Fadil, when you get back home, I need you to start looking around about a job for me in Saudi Arabia. Something flexible. Something that doesn't require me being there all day. Find something for Azad too. It needs to be an American company. I'm going to make sure Prince Mussab is willing to vouch for us when we meet up this weekend. I'm pretty sure Gina will be working him too. Some of the things the Prince said tonight make me think something is going down. He almost spilled the beans and Peter stopped me. He was right, if I had pressed him at the time, he may have shut down. Whatever he was about to say, we need to find out what it is. Do the Knights have other assets in Saudi Arabia at this time? I'm probably going to need some help. I'm not sure how much, but I'll keep you informed." "Yes," Fadil said. "I don't know exactly how many or where they are but I'll track them down. What are your plans?"

"I don't know for sure yet. It's just a hunch. I'd like to stay there for at least six weeks or so."

"Will do Jonathan. Give me a few days. I'll get back to you."

Jonathan went back to his room and looked up Kathlen's phone number. It was 2:30 am in Cyprus. He wasn't sure where she would be on her U.S. to Germany route or if she was off that day. It would either be around 8 pm in Atlanta or 2:30 am if she was in Germany. Now was as good a time to call her as any. "Hello," she answered.

"Hey, this is Jonathan. Did I wake you?"

"No," she replied. "I was up watching some TV. Where are you? Are you back from Cyprus?"

"No," he said. "I'll be here probably until next week."

"Are you having fun?" she asked. "Yeah, it was good hanging out with the guys. I was thinking about asking you to come down...if you're not working or don't have plans." He was hoping she didn't and he wouldn't have to spend an hour convincing her. He waited.

"Hmm, for how long?" she asked. "Well, at least for the weekend. Longer if you can. We can maybe leave together if you can stay that long."

She paused again. "I think I can do that. Let's play it by ear and just say the weekend for now. You may want to kick me out after a few days."

"Why, do you snore?" Jonathan kidded.

"If you're not nice to me, you won't find out...will you?" she said.

Jonathan laughed. "You got me. I'll be on my best behavior. Can you come in on Friday afternoon? A friend is having a party on his boat. He's a nice guy. Kind of lonely. I'm going to hook him up with one of my friends from Italy. She's a nice girl. I think they'll like each other."

"So, am I going to be your date for this party?" she asked.

"Maybe if you're nice to me," Jonathan said. He stayed on a while longer with her flirting and for the first time in a long time, he was starting to feel something. Something he hadn't felt in a long time.

Jonathan didn't wake up until almost noon. He wondered if he had missed any messages. He checked. All was quiet. Fadil had probably left. Peter and Azad were probably still asleep or nursing a hangover. Later that afternoon, he caught up with them. They both came by his room. Jonathan discussed his note to Julie, his instructions to Fadil, his conversation and date with Kathlen and the need to contact Gina, their operative in Italy. He thanked Peter for keeping him from rushing head first into an interrogation of the Prince the night before. He told them in general about his plans. He left it up to Peter to contact Gina and set things up for that weekend. Jonathan really hadn't spent much time getting to know Gina. He met her while having drinks in a bar in Italy with a few other Knights. She was a knockout but he was quietly informed that she was one of them. She wasn't actively working in the field anymore chasing bad guys but neither had she officially retired. Most Knights didn't. It was a brotherhood where one didn't have to retire; they could just say no when asked to participate in an operation. He was also told to stay away from her if he didn't want his heart broken and handed to him. It was tempting. Gina was beautiful and smart. Jonathan wasn't sure if her art business had been a cover for her before or after she joined the Knights but she apparently was doing pretty well for herself from what he could tell. When Jonathan was talking to the Prince and was trying to come up with someone for him to meet, he instantly thought of Gina. Hopefully, she wouldn't break the poor guy's heart until after they got what they needed. Peter also had met her a few times over the years and knew her a little better than Jonathan. Peter agreed to take a hop over to Italy and talk to her. Later that evening, Peter took the short flight from Cyprus to Italy. He met with her in her office in the gallery the next morning. "To what do I owe the honor of your visit Peter?" she asked.

"Just what we discussed last night. I know you're not that into us anymore," Peter joked.

"Don't be silly Peter. I'm still family. What do we have?" she asked.

Peter discussed the plans with her for the next hour. Afterwards, he asked if one day was enough to prepare. "Under normal circumstances, we'd have a file for you but you're going to have to follow your instincts to a certain extent and play this one by ear." Peter told her.

"Don't worry Peter. I'll be there on Friday afternoon. When you get back, either you or Jonathan call me and give me anything else you may know or find out. I'll make some calls and do some research myself."

Gina arrived early Friday evening and met Peter in the hotel lobby. They took the elevator up to Jonathan's room. Jonathan and Azad were waiting for them. Jonathan filled her in on their mission. After the short meeting, Gina went to check in and go over her notes. Peter and Azad left together to decide who would be the least obnoxious girls to take with them as dates.

Chapter Twenty-Seven

Jonathan checked the time and decided to leave a little early for the airport to pick up Kathlen. He went down stairs and asked the clerk to call up a limousine. He found Kathlen's gate and took a seat to wait for the plane from Germany to arrive. Passengers soon started walking through the gates. Jonathan stood up as he saw her walking down the ramp towards him. She looked as beautiful to him as the day he met her on the plane—just more casually dressed with her long flowing brown hair down past her shoulders. *Nice* Jonathan thought. *I can see myself with her.* She walked over to him. Jonathan had been so busy looking at her that he forgot to think of something clever to say. The only thing that came out of his mouth as he grabbed her hands was, "Wow, I think I missed you. I'm glad you're here." It caught her off guard. She let go of his hands and hugged him. "I am too. I had not expected you to call until you got back to the States but I'm really happy to see you. Weird."

"Weird?" Jonathan asked.

"No, not in a bad way. It's just that I wasn't prepared for this. I mean meeting someone after..." Jonathan interrupted her. "There's time. I'm sure there's as much about me that you want to know as I want to know about you. We've got the whole weekend, maybe a little longer. The limo's waiting." Back at the hotel, Jonathan handed Kathlen the key to her room. "Do you want to go to your room and relax for a bit, walk out to the beach, or get a massage down the hall or what do you have in mind?" he asked.

"Can we go to your room and talk?" she said.

"Sure but remember, I'm a guy. Housekeeping was here earlier but I've got a few things lying around." She waved off the idea. Jonathan had forgotten to turn the TV off before leaving. He turned the channel from U.S. news and started scrolling the music channels. "What type of music do you like?" he asked.

"Oh, if I have a choice, I kind of like old school R&B or soul. What about you?"

"Same here," he said. "There's nothing like Marvin Gaye, Luther, even Sam Cooke." She agreed. "Especially Sam Cooke. I remember my mom, when she used to cook she'd dance around the kitchen listening to him and some of those other guys," she wistfully told him. Jonathan said, "I grew up in Germany. My mom is German. It was my dad playing the R&B and soul. My mom likes some of it. I guess they used to go dancing on base." They continued talking for hours. They walked out on the balcony.

That's where they kissed. They went back inside and ordered room service and continued talking about their lives. Jonathan hinted at what he did but didn't give her too many details and she didn't ask for any. She just asked if he'd promise her to stay safe for her. He promised he would.

Chapter Twenty-Eight

Jonathan called Prince Mussab and told him everything was set up for the following day. "Even the Italian girl you mentioned?" the Prince asked. "Yes she arrived today, luckily she was free for the weekend, and even Peter and Azad found dates. They invited two girls from the club," Jonathan answered. "What about the young lady you met?" Mussab replied. "She is here. It should be fun. Adan, my company is paying me well but I am still into traveling and exploring the world. Is Saudi Arabia a place you think I'd like?" Jonathan laid the groundwork. "Sure Jonathan," the Prince answered. "You would love it. If something comes up let me know and I will put in a good word for you."

"Thank you, Prince I appreciate that. It was just a thought and we have to talk more about it one day," With that Jonathan ended the conversation.

The limo pulled up to Prince's floating castle. Jonathan, his friends and their respective dates were met by Mussab's bodyguards who announced their arrival by walkie-talkie. "Your guests have arrived, Your Highness." They escorted the group aboard where the Prince graciously greeted them. "Welcome to my humble home." The Prince was all smiles. Jonathan introduced him to Gina, Kathlen and the two other girls that Peter and Azad brought as dates. They were offered drinks and hors d' oeuvres and after a few minutes were ushered to a banquet table. During dinner Jonathan noticed that Gina and the Prince were very interested in each other. Kathlen also seemed to be enjoying herself. After dinner Peter and Azad took their dates to the rear deck to lounge, chat and enjoy the beautiful view of the twinkling lights of the city reflecting on the water. A perfect setting for a date. Jonathan and Kathlen stayed with Gina and the Prince for a while and then excused themselves to join the others on the rear deck.

The Prince asked Gina to join him in the yacht's living room where they sat down on oversized sofas. "So, do you have children?" The Prince could not wait to find out more about this beautiful woman, so he felt he might as well come right out and ask direct questions. "No," she replied "I've never been married and have no children. I guess I never had enough time to meet the right person. What about you, what should I call you?" "Call me?" the Prince asked confused. "I mean is Prince your first name, do you allow people to call you by your first name?" He felt foolish. "No, I understand. My name is Adan, Adan Mussab." She went on to interrogate. "Do you have children or have ever been married?" "No," he replied. "I have spent most of the last few years in the U.S. getting my Doctorate degree."

"I went to college for a few years but I like to work and my gallery is a big part of me."

"Jonathan told me you owned a gallery; are you an artist?" the Prince asked.

"No, my grandfather was. He started the business and my father who was also an artist took it over after my grandfather died and I am in the line of succession." She had been looking at the paintings on the wall and then asked, "Can I take a look at that painting?" "Sure", he said. She walked over to the picture on the wall "Is it on alarm?" She looked at him questioningly. He shook his head. She turned over the smallest of the three paintings and smiled. "You have good taste Adan; this one is from my gallery." The Prince walked over to see what she was talking about and on the back of the picture the gold label said "Francello Gallery". He thought it was odd. "I see that you like Italian styling," Gina kidded him. "More than you know," he said as he looked deep into her eyes. Their conversation was cut short as the others joined them in the living room since it was getting cooler on the deck. Soon after everybody said that they had a wonderful time, and called it a night. For Prince Mussab the evening was coming to an end too quickly. While saying their goodbyes Adan asked Gina if she had to leave for Italy the next day. She told him that she wanted to enjoy the island for a few days. He asked if he could join her. "Only if it's my treat next time Adan," she said. "Can I call you tomorrow?" he asked.

"Sure, I am staying at the same hotel as my friends. You can call me there." With that she walked away to join her friends in the limo.

Just as Jonathan expected, the Prince called him within an hour after they arrived back at their hotel. "Jonathan, she is fantastic." The Prince sounded excited. "Thank you for introducing us. She told me she would like to see the island and I want to make that a great experience. Do you have any ideas what she might like?"

"No problem Prince," Jonathan answered calmly all the while thinking how well his plan was working. "Why don't you take in some museums and galleries and have lunch at a quiet bistro? That it something I would do on a first date. Gina is not your ordinary girl."

 "I know Jonathan and I am sorry for taking up your time. I know you have a special person with you." "Yeah, she is here," Jonathan said. "We are trying to get to know each other and we are having a great time doing so".

"Thank you again Jonathan. I will call Gina and let you go," The Prince ended the conversation.

Gina and Adan spent the weekend getting to know each other as did Jonathan and Kathlen. The following week they all prepared to leave the island, for it was time to get back to work. Before leaving the island, Prince and Jonathan had a chance to talk. Adan really liked Gina and he reiterated his ability to help should Jonathan decide to come to Saudi Arabia for employment. Azad and Peter went to their respective countries after promising to keep in touch to do this again. Jonathan and Kathlen travelled to Germany. He had promised his mother that he'd stop in to see grandma and he asked Kathlen to go with him and then travel to San Antonio to meet his family. She agreed.

"Hey Pap, how are you? Good. It was great; my friends and I had a good time. Are you okay? Good, can I speak to Mom?" His mother got on the phone.

"Hey Mom, just wanted to let you know I am going to stop in to see Grandma and bring your stuff. It was fine. Mom, I am bringing a special friend home to meet you all and no she is not a mermaid. Her name is Kathlen. See you soon and I love you both; give

Dad a hug from me." Jonathan could not wait to see his parents to introduce Kathlen. He was excited; this was not like him. He felt unfamiliar emotions.

Chapter Twenty-Nine

The next day Jonathan received a call from Fadil. "Jonathan where are you?"

"I am in Germany with Kathlen visiting relatives, what's up?" Jonathan answered.

"There is a lot of chatter. Have you seen it? It is not the usual terrorist chatter. Something big is going down in Saudi Arabia. They're up to something. Not sure what yet," Fadil continued.

"No, I guess I have to get out of vacation mode. I'll contact Gina and see if she has anything yet. We left and she stayed behind with Mussab." The call ended. He messaged Gina. "Lots of chatter in Saudi. What is it?" Gina was still in Cyprus. She actually enjoyed herself with the Prince but she had never let her feelings get in the way of her job and duty to her homeland, its freedoms and people. She wasn't going to start now. She spent time with the Prince touring the island. She actually liked him. When they were having lunch on the yacht he asked her. "Gina if we were going to take this relationship further would you be interested in moving to Saudi Arabia?" Her reaction was forceful and quick. "No, there is no way I would move to Saudi Arabia. Your treatment of women is not something I could put up with. Saudi Arabia does not have a good track record when it comes to civil rights. I am sorry, I think you are a nice guy but I could never live in Saudi Arabia." The Prince was silent. "What if I moved if something were to come of us?" Gina added. "So you mean Italy?" The Prince cautiously replied. "Yes, Italy, as my family is there. I wouldn't mind traveling but living in the Middle East? No way!" Gina realized she might have risked her mission but he caught her by surprise with his question and she had always expressed her feelings as she saw fit. She watched the Prince, who seemed deep in thought and then he spoke. "Gina, I really like you. I've met many women but none like you. I would be willing to live in Italy. I travel a lot and it would not be a big deal for me." She was surprised. "What about your family and your standing?" she asked. "I don't think I would be the first man to leave home for love. Of course they would not like it but as far as my standing no one can change that. Saudi Arabia as you say is not fair. There are people who are very unhappy with the Royal Family because of the way they are treated. It seems though that the family wants to do more to take away people's rights." He hesitated but Gina wanted to keep this conversation going as it was just what she needed. "What do you mean?" She looked at him questioningly. He continued. "There are people that are brought to Saudi Arabia for work; they are not always treated fairly. I personally would like for Saudis to have more freedoms. I spent most of my adult life in Western nations and I would like to see my country become more open, more tolerant but..." he hesitated again. "But what?" Gina pushed on. "The leaders of Western nations are addicted to Saudi oil and money that does not help." "Who are these corrupt leaders?" She bluntly asked. "Well your President for one but he is not the only one. Leaders from around the world are getting paid off for looking the other way when things are done that their citizens don't like. I don't think this is a secret." *No it's not a secret; where is he going with this?* She asked herself. But he was on a roll. It appeared he was trying to get this off his chest. "Sharia Law is not just in the Middle East. Informally it is set up in many nations under the guise of religious freedom. These officials allow it and the church leaders are quiet. This bothers me. Let me give you some history. There are Sunnis and there are Shiites." Gina knew that but she was not going to interrupt him. "The modern kingdom of Saudi Arabia was formed in 1932 between the House of Saud and followers of a strict Islamic secular, Muhammed ibn Addal-Wahhab. We are therefore

Wahhabi. Wahhabis are in the minority in terms of population but they control all religious institutions, courts and education. It is mostly the Shiites in Saudi Arabia who are unhappy. As far as who is more anti-Israel, I don't know. It appears to be all of the above. Although my family and Saudi Arabia rely on the protection of the United States and Israel, they secretly support their destruction and fund it. I guess I am more secular in nature. I believe that religion and governance of people should be separate from one's personal views about religion." "What are you going to do about it Adan?" Gina asked. He looked very surprised at her question. "What do you think I can do? I am only one person; that is the way it has been for many years and those who do not agree with the family live abroad but still accept their actions. There is not much choice. They are also addicted to the money and what else could they do? With the far reach the Saudi family has all over the word they would not be able to get a job or even start a business." Gina decided to accept his invitation to take her to Italy on the yacht instead of her flying back home. The trip was short but joyful. Before the Prince could embark to Italy he received a message to come home to attend to some business dealings. He was disappointed but duty called. "Gina, I am being called home, I will not be able to spend some time with you in Italy. I must get back."

"What's wrong Adan?" Gina asked.

"There is a meeting I would rather not be part of. It is related to the things I have been talking to you about. I cannot tell you any more than that but I may not attend. I don't know." They said their goodbyes and he kissed her while telling her he would be back as soon as he could. Gina left the boat and while she was traveling to her home by taxi she called Jonathan. "Gina here, you need to get to Saudi Arabia ASAP. There is a meeting going on in a few days by the Saudi family. All I know so far that it is a planning meeting."

"I know, I've been talking to Fadil and some of our guys. Something is going down. Do you have any more info?" Jonathan asked.

"All I know is that the family is having a meeting. Adan didn't give me any details and I did not want to push him. He told me he would be back soon I will find out more then." Gina sounded disappointed in herself. "Don't worry about it; Fadil is working on getting a job for me and Azad in Saudi Arabia. What I suspect is that the Saudis are playing both sides of the coin. They are paying off world leaders on the one hand while sneaking billions of dollars and weapons to various terror groups out the back door. What we must find out is when the next meeting is that is the important one." Jonathan felt anxious; he knew he had to get to Saudi Arabia. "What happens at the next meeting?" Gina was not very curious. "I am pretty sure that's when the rubber hits the road. The Saudis are not working on a nuke. The same people they are funding to help conquer the West are the same terrorist organizations that want the Caliphate themselves. At the next meeting it's payday. They will sit across the table with some of the most important government leaders and church leaders, look them in the eye and ask them for a commitment to allow Sharia Law. After that they are going to cut some fat checks. We need to know the names of those in attendance and how much they are getting paid for selling out their countrymen. The next time you meet Adan you need to press him hard."

There was silence on the other end. "You like him don't you?" Jonathan asked.

"Sure, I like him but I love Italy," she quickly answered.

"I know you do Gina. I am not questioning your loyalty. I know what it means to like someone. Just see if you can get anything on it. No one will ever question your loyalty. I'd be silly to question how important it is to be human and liking someone. I am learning this myself. Adan seems to be a nice guy, just be careful."

"Thank you Jonathan," she said.

"Thank you for what," was his reply.

"Thank you for all you do and thank you for being human."

"Gina, I am not James Bond. I am a Knight just like you." With that they ended their conversation.

Chapter Thirty

Later that day Fadil answered Jonathan's message. He sent an encrypted e-mail. 'Hey Jonathan, I got you on at a chemical company, kind of'. Jonathan answered back, 'What do you mean, kind of?' Fadil was on the computer and they switched to their secret communication mode. 'There is a company called Epic. It's a chemical company, and there is a weak link. Their human resources director is looking around for jobs in the U.S. He is probably sick of being away from his family and of Saudi in general.' 'I am on it Fadil. I know someone who can contact him. What kind of money is he looking for?'

'He's making $200,000 right now,' Fadil replied. 'Not a problem Fadil. I'll call my friend and make arrangements. What else you got?' Jonathan asked. 'Well, we still have the Saudis sending arms to Al Qaeda and to another group that is emerging. Poor guys they are caught between a rock and a hard place.' Jonathan responded, 'Yeah I know, they have the Shiites in Iran working with Russia on one side and they've been extorted by Al Qaeda and the group of Sunnis on the other side. At the same time, they're depending on the US for protection. The same U.S. that their religion requires them to subjugate or kill.' 'You've got it Jonathan,' Fadil replied. Jonathan was on a roll; he felt something inside of him that gave him strength. 'We need to get the original documents, laptop or tablet with these people's names. We need to find out who is heading that meeting. When we have the information we can send it to Julie. We can put pressure on these leaders to resign with that. In some cases we may have to do a little more than put pressure on.' Fadil asked, 'What about President Corona? We can't take out the most powerful man in the world, can we?' Jonathan thought for a moment. 'Fadil, find me a couple of our brothers. Arrange for them to meet Azad and me once you find out who will have the documents.' 'Meet you where Jonathan?' Fadil asked. "Whenever you have the names of the people with the information Azad and I will have to take it from there. I will give you further information at that time. In the meantime find me reliable brothers who are able to go home after their mission. I need to come up with a good plan. I will talk to you soon." Fadil and Jonathan ended their conversation after some small talk about Cyprus. Just flying into Saudi Arabia was easy enough; he had done it on many occasions. One thing about governments—few ever check anything, however they want you to think they do. When someone gets caught doing something they're not supposed to do (depending on who it is), they're usually made an example of and in Saudi Arabia there was little room for error. Azad was already in place. Jonathan decided to leave Peter out of this mission. They couldn't take a chance with Peter's accent and white skin. He would stand out. Other Knight family members had been brought in and were secretly and quietly going about their daily lives. They worked for other American companies in Saudi Arabia or they blended in with all the other U.S. personnel there flying in and out of Europe and the United States. These men would serve as eyes and ears for Fadil, Johnathan and Azad.

EPIC Chemicals was respected and trusted by the Saudi government. The primary reason was because the family really had no idea what EPIC did except they knew they manufactured products using oil by-products such as polymers, chemicals and fertilizers. These were subjects that were not of much interest to the Royal Family. Their interest was that the company made their kingdom money and lots of it. The Saudi Family cut a brilliant deal in 1976 when the company contacted them about opening there. They felt that they had taken the lion's share of profits from the infidel businessmen.

The business was a good fit for the Saudis. They could make huge profits off the by-product of the oil of which they had so much. Jonathan had discussed the job opportunity with Prince Mussab while in Cyprus. The Prince had no problem making the necessary calls to get Jonathan hired.

It wasn't easy to go unnoticed in Saudi Arabia without being suspected of something. Creating an opening as a manager had required a little assistance on Jonathan's part. The current manager had only been on the job for two years so Jonathan had to speed up the process. He contacted a friend who owned a private company in the United States and made him an offer. He told him that he needed to create an opening in Epic's Human Resources Department; that meant his friend would need to recruit this guy and hire him.

Jonathan told his friend that he would be willing to pay the person a salary for five years at $250,000 per year plus a bonus for him. Jonathan's friend agreed to hire whomever Jonathan had in mind with the understanding that after two years he could let the person go and keep the extra money. Jonathan called the banker and had him wire $250,000 dollars to his friend who assured him there would be an opening at EPIC by the end of the month.

Within a week, someone from Epic was contacting Jonathan telling him that there was an unexpected opening as manager in the Human Resources Department. The previous manager had been contacted by a headhunter back in the United States offering him a job at $200,000 per year. He told Jonathan that the job was his if he wanted it. Jonathan asked the caller if he could sleep on it. Somewhere along the way $50,000 per year had been siphoned off the poor guy that had left Epic. He had taken the job at two hundred thousand a year whereas if he had a held out a bit he could have at fifty-thousand more. Jonathan chuckled to himself and thought the poor guy must have had enough of Saudi Arabia; he most likely was homesick as Fadil suspected.

It had been a long flight from the United States but Jonathan couldn't say it was uncomfortable. It didn't come as a surprise to him; there were a lot of things he had researched about his new company and he made himself familiar with their dealings. He couldn't afford to make a mistake or get one of his guys killed.

During the initial call, the person on the other end of the phone didn't know anything about him except what he had told them, what was on his resume and that Prince Mussad had given him a letter of reference. He was told that the company had a private plane bringing over eleven other employees that Saturday morning or he could wait until the following month, if there were loose ends that he needed to wrap up in the States. He already knew that. He also knew the people that he'd be flying with and two of them were his men from the Knights. They had coordinated the move with him and Fadil. The other travelers on the plane had been researched and information on each had been given to Jonathan.

There was nothing extraordinary about any of them, except for a lone female passenger. From the picture he had, she looked to be Asian. She had gone to MIT with an undergraduate in Chemistry and a Master's degree in Applied Science. The other passengers and future employees of Epic were all men and were all who they said they were. All were just looking to find a better life abroad for a few years. None of course would have admitted that to whoever hired them. That might have killed their chances of getting the job. He told his interviewer from Epic that he was single and there wasn't really any reason he couldn't be on the next flight. He told Jonathan there would be a concierge contacting him shortly and that everything he needed would be taken care of. His transportation, his housing, food and car or driver would all be paid for each month by the company. Jonathan thanked him for the opportunity and in conclusion the man gave Jonathan his direct number in case of further questions. He then said, "Thank you Mr. Knight and welcome to Epic Chemicals."

People were always curious about his last name being Knight. They never realized the symbolism of the name he had adopted. This family of modern-day Knights of the Temple had grown into a worldwide force equal to or greater than that of any government; he was often asked if he was related to Gladys Knight. His answer was always simple "No, I wish I was, I wouldn't have to work as hard." Little did any of them know that the man they talked to was actively engaged in saving them and others from a global conspiracy? He then thought to himself that he would rather be asked that question a million times more than anyone suspecting anything about him. Jonathan knew that they wouldn't understand even if he did tell them. It wasn't like a once in a while thing that he often found himself on dangerous missions. Maybe it was the prayers that he heard from those who were suffering that made him continue. Prayers that were meant for God, but he somehow heard them first.

Chapter Thirty-One

Epic's American compound was a city within a city. Actually it was outside the city. It was sort of like a subdivision of Riyadh when Jonathan was in the Kingdom before he stayed at the military compound. This was different. Fadil had sent him pictures. There were no soldiers or religious police patrolling the area. It looked like normal houses on normal streets. There were grocery stores and convenient stores and all homes had Internet. Jonathan's house was furnished nicely. Obviously Epic Chemical was doing well. Everything he needed was there. All he had to do was unpack his suitcase. He had all day to get the lay of the neighborhood before starting work the next day. He just needed to remember, even though this place looked like a modern American city, it was still Saudi Arabia.

The Middle East was not an easy place to understand even for people who live there. It was a constantly changing region of the world that never really moved forward. Every day seemed to be Groundhog Day as people went to work and back home. Even though cities were built and outward things seemed to modernize the life for people in the region freedoms stayed the same. A sense of hopelessness couldn't really be described because to feel hopelessness one would need to first experience hope. In a life without hope, the experience would be like being born without sight. Without sight a person would never attempt to look for the gold at the end of a rainbow because they would not know what a rainbow looked like. There is a big difference between someone describing a rainbow and actually seeing one. This was the experience for most in the Middle East that Jonathan came across while living and working there. There was a big difference between the natives that never traveled and those who had. The hardliners knew this. They knew that the King's loyalty to Islam was to prevent the followers from seeing the rainbow and being tempted by any bad earthly beauty. They blindly obeyed to assure their eventual award of life everlasting as described by their prophet. Any interference from the outside world was unwanted. Any interference would be an affront to their very existence in their quest for spirit hood and Allah's promise to them of eternal salvation. Anything that was an affront to their deeply felt personal faith was evil—even something as innocent as an aid worker from another nation trying to help. A reporter innocently trying to tell their story might present the possibility for their people to hear about the beauty of the rainbow and ultimately convince a Muslim to try to pursue the pot of gold at the end of it. This, in their mind would cause the ruination of their people and straying from Allah.

People in the Western World would never understand these deeply held beliefs. The thought of seeing beauty as being counterproductive just wasn't something they could comprehend. If someone in the Western World sees beauty they want to describe it, explain it, chase it, possess it and cherish owning it. If someone else was missing out on it they would describe the missing parts. If the other person was interested in learning about the beauty, no big deal either. The idea of remaining blind for spiritual reasons just isn't reasonable for Western ways. If a person chooses to remain blind, that is their choice. In the Middle East if a person chooses to see they may get stoned to death.

As Jonathan checked out his new temporary home his thoughts wondered to the situation back home. They had elected President Corona. Who was he? What person in their right mind would come along and attempt to change 239 years of history in the most powerful nation on earth? Who had gone through the enormous task of preventing voters from really knowing anything about him or at least the truth about him? These were questions no one could seem to answer or at least had the courage to ask. Jonathan saw Corona's cabinet go from radical to extreme radical. Almost every Federal Agency Director from the IRS to the EPA was handpicked to obey orders and they did. Corona was free to use the power of these agencies to reward his friends or punish his political enemies. Things seemed to have gotten too far out of control for Jonathan to understand. His friends at the FBI were also on pins and needles. They could no longer call a spade a spade without risking their entire career and their financial security. His own agency, the CIA, was not quite as nervous but the tensions were thick. No one knew whom to trust. They had witnessed long-term career agents and four-star generals at the Pentagon fired unceremoniously like part-time workers at Walmart. Voters did not realize the damage they had done—at least not most of them. Prior to Corona's election, Jonathan did not pay much attention to politics but that changed with the election. His brothers and sisters at the Knight family knew who he was and so did the CIA but could do little about it except watch voters make one of the biggest mistakes in U.S. history.

The planning of Corona's advance team was extensive and the results were quick. After the election they set their plans in place to let the economy flounder. His campaign promises to lower taxes on the middle class, were lies. It was unclear to Jonathan who the exact people were that had the greatest influence on Corona or which government had given the most money to help groom him and his quick accent to the Presidency. It may have been Saudi Arabia, Russia, China—any combination of those or others. What was clear was at the peril of the United States, he had made some pretty big promises to a lot of people. What was amazing to Jonathan and many in the intelligence community was how he was able to keep juggling so many balls for so long with very few missteps. Nothing ever stuck on him. Between the media covering for him, his lack of conscience and his always being able to hit the right notes on his teleprompter, he was able to stage scandals and make mistakes that no other President in history had been able to make without consequences. Whoever he was working with had planned this internal coup of the government for a long time. It was an orchestrated effort from seemingly the entire Democratic Party, the Liberal Media and another group, government or organization that wanted to change the United States. Whoever that missing piece was had very deep pockets. Some rumored it was the shadowy group called the illuminati, a group of the wealthiest billionaires in the world with the resources at their fingertips to control world leaders and governments. He was not sure who it was, just like it was not known that the Knights Templar still existed. They had to fight. Sometimes all they could do was manage and clean up the mess afterwards. Finding the source of the mess was often much more difficult. Whole industries were turned upside down. The financial industry, healthcare and energy industries were first. Corona went after the Second Amendment trying to ban guns, and the First Amendment by setting up "Free Speech zones" during protests and attempts to regulate the Internet. Surprisingly, Corona's supporters remained loyal to him as if they were under a spell. They became thoughtless zombies. The media continued to feed them misinformation and they believed. It seemed few of them could see where they are being led. Too few knew enough history and were destined to repeat it even if it literally enslaved or killed them. Jonathan was deep in thought when someone tapped him on the shoulder.

"Hey old buddy what's up? It was Azad, who had arrived earlier and was trying to get acquainted with his new home just like Jonathan. The two friends walked down the street together talking about their concerns.

Chapter Thirty-Two

Steve was asked to come down to the police station. Christian prepped him on what to expect. He just wasn't sure if this was going to turn into a media circus if Julie wasn't found soon. What was he supposed to do, go down to the station and tell them the government kidnapped his wife? He hired an attorney to make the call and go with him. He knew either way he'd be a suspect with or without a lawyer. After they returned from the station, he knew he was right. Christian, Angela and Sarah agreed to stay with him at his house. They knew they were all better off being together but they also knew both the local police and the government would be watching them come and go. At least this way, the government wouldn't come after any of them as long as the local cops were watching Steve. The local cops were no fans of liberalism or of President Franklin Corona. Christian knew it was time to contact Jonathan and then contact and alert their team members to let them know about Julie.

The war had started with Julie's kidnapping. Although Julie had lost track of how long she'd been held captive, she knew her team would be working on finding her but she didn't know that much about Jonathan. She just knew that he was probably the reason she was here, wherever 'here' was. He hadn't yet gone into great details with her on what his plans to save the world were—but he had pissed off some pretty important people and they thought she was in on it.

When Jonathan got the message from Christian, he wasn't surprised. He was expecting it. He knew someone had gone through Julie's computer looking for what they thought he had sent her. The guys from NSA had been tracking the Knights for several years. They hadn't improved much. It still seemed like they were hiring kids off the street as long as they were able to hack a computer. Obviously, Julie's rise to prominence must have made someone in Corona's cabinet nervous. After putting a kid from NSA on the case, the next thing would be to contact someone from CIA or a Black Ops unit and put them on notice. Jonathan knew they had nothing on him or the Knights. All they had was a message where they couldn't break the encryption from someone they couldn't trace. But, they had Julie. Jonathan typed a quick message to Christian, "I pretty much know where she is and who has her. Stay put. Keep her husband calm and only tell those who need to know. She'll be home soon." The NSA agents were amateurs. They left things in Julie's computer that a ninth grader could find. Their encryption was from the 1990s. Their programmers were guys who wrote code before Y2K.

Chapter Thirty-Three

Jonathan couldn't leave his job in Saudi for long. He had only been there a few days but he would help. The Knights would help Julie. He knew she couldn't be far from home. He knew the government had her. If they were going to move her, it would be by plane. Anything else could draw too much attention and they wouldn't want that. Fox News would have a field day with that kind of information. The closest and most private military base was Camp Stanley. Camp Bullis was an adjacent post used for training. It was too busy. So was Randolph Air Force Base. Plus Randolph was across town. The government was kidnapping a prominent U.S citizen. The most private and quickest place to take her was Camp Stanley. Very few people knew much about Camp Stanley. Many, including the Mayor of San Antonio didn't know the base was still being actively used by the CIA to conduct Black Ops missions, delivering weapons and pallets of money to foreign fighters, developing and storing chemical weapons and obviously now making citizens disappear. Nothing like kidnapping a U.S. citizen had ever happened but who knew the depths to which Corona would stoop. Stanley also had holding cells and an interrogation facility. Jonathan started making calls when he arrived at his house. "Hello Adan, how are you? I am sorry to bother you but I need another favor. I am sorry but my father has taken ill and I need to go home to see him. I know I only got here a few days ago but he is getting older and I don't ever want to miss saying goodbye to him."

"Nice to hear from you Jonathan; don't worry I will arrange everything. How long will you be gone? I have not had the time to even welcome you here," the Prince replied.

"Yes, I am sorry. Hopefully, I will not be gone more than two weeks. I just want to make sure everything is fine and he does not need more than my mother can provide. I hope you understand." Jonathan tried to sound very concerned which was not hard; he was concerned about Julie. He knew the Saudis would call his home but his mother answered the phone most of the time and she knew if a stranger called for his father he was too sick to come to the phone.

"I will talk to your company immediately and I will make sure your papers are in order for re-entry in the Kingdom. Take care of you father; maybe someday I will meet him." The Prince was very helpful and happy to hear Jonathan's voice. "Thank you Prince, I owe you one." Jonathan hung up the phone to start making arrangements for his trip to the US. He didn't want to get too many people involved, alarm whoever was holding her and give them a reason to move her. If she was at Stanley, J.R. would know. J.R. was a good man. He was a long-time civilian employee at Stanley. He didn't want to drop this on him in a phone call; he'd have to do it in person. The Prince would take care of the emergency leave from the job. He called his father and told him that this was one of these times when he needed help. "I hate to do this dad," he said. I need you to be sick so I can get back to the States to take care of a problem that the government created. I need cover in case someone calls. Let Mom answer the phone for a few days. You're too sick and can't come to the phone."

"You know we have your back, son," his dad replied. The Prince's aide called his parents' home as expected, and asked for Jonathan's father. When he was told he was too sick to come to the phone the papers were expedited the next day.

Chapter Thirty-Four

Only his team in the Knights and Christian knew he was in San Antonio. He knew where J.R. lived. He had been invited to his home to celebrate his daughter's sixteenth birthday. In the Hispanic community, the sixteenth birthday celebration when he worked at Camp Stanley. The sixteenth birthday is was usually reserved for family and close friends and was a special occasion. To J.R., Jonathan was almost family. He and Jonathan had become friends while Jonathan was on assignment at Camp Stanley. As a long-time employee, J.R. showed Jonathan the lay of the land. No one really knew what J.R.'s job title was. He wore a lot of hats. He was the maintenance man, delivery man, supervisor, groundskeeper and unofficial head of security. At some point, some government bureaucrat had decided that a bunch of military and CIA guys carrying guns didn't need a security company getting in the way or sticking their noses into anything. Therefore, J.R. became the camp's jack of all trades long before Jonathan ever got there. He was a great guy, loyal to a fault and a hard worker; he just had one problem. He liked to drink but he was always functional. Although the top brass at the camp loved him, having someone that literally walked around the post carrying the keys to the candy store, getting charged with DUI's wasn't a good thing. At one point, Jonathan had to get up in the middle of the night to bail him out of jail and take him home. His wife wasn't very happy. Neither was his supervisor at Stanley who was going to fire him until Jonathan interceded and talked J.R. into going to rehab. Jonathan picked up his phone and found J.R.'s number. "Hey, J.R. what's up friend?"

"Jonathan, where the hell are you? How are you?"

"Fine man. I'm in the area. Got a few minutes?"

"Hell yeah man. Come on by." Jonathan wasn't far from J.R.'s house, so within ten minutes he was on his friend's porch knocking on the door. When J.R. answered, they hugged like pals that hadn't seen each other for years and they hadn't. "Where's the family?" Jonathan asked him. "The wife took the kids to visit her mom down in Brownsville for the weekend. I had to work. Want a drink? I'm drinking Mountain Dew." "Sure, I'll take a bottle of water. Hey look, I'll shoot straight with you. I'm looking for a lady. She went missing a few days ago. I got a hunch she's at Stanley." J.R. paused. "Probably the lady I'm feeding. I don't know much about her though. I just take food and clean clothes to her cell, Who is she?" he asked.

"She's a journalist. I'm working with her and I think Corona grabbed her." Jonathan replied.

J.R.'s jaw dropped. "Son of a bitch. She's there. I deliver her food every day. I had no idea."

"Who would know J. R.? Who would expect this from our government? You know I'm going to have to take her right?"

J.R. looked at him and asked, "But your job?"

"They won't know. You won't know. Right?" Jonathan looked at him and winked.

"Of course not Jonathan. You're my brother. What can I do to help?" J.R. said sheepishly.

"Unless things have changed drastically, there's only a handful of people on Stanley at any given time. Here's what I need for you to do." J.R. knew what Jonathan wanted him to do and it probably would come at some risk. He had never been a political guy but he was a righteous guy. He had honorably served in the army during a relatively peaceful time period. He had grown up on the southwest side of San Antonio. He volunteered to get out of San Antonio, travel and see the world. He never made it outside of Texas. He did his basic training in Killeen, less than 200 miles away. After basic, he was stationed back in San Antonio. He married his high school sweetheart and did a four-year stint. He landed the job at Stanley shortly afterwards. "Whatever you need Jonathan. I never talked to her but if what you're saying is true, it's wrong. Whatever I need to do. I trust you." Jonathan jokingly asked him, "Do you still remember what I taught you on how to pass a lie detector test? You're probably going to have to take one when they find you tied up. By the way, how are your daughter Maria and your son Louis? Are they in college?"

J.R. replied, "Only part-time. I wasn't able to save much for them because of all the legal fees."

"Have them apply for full-time. I'll have a scholarship set aside for them. When you're ready to retire, call me."

"Jonathan, you know you don't have to do this but thank you friend. I know not to ask you details but when is this happening?"

Jonathan answered, "Tomorrow. Do the guys there still go to lunch around the same time?" The answer was affirmative. "You won't have to do much. Just act surprised and let them tie you up. You won't even have to get roughed up. First off, they're doing something illegal. It's not like they're going to put out an APB for us or drum you out. Plus, they wouldn't expect a fifty-two-year-old man working nearly by himself to put up a big struggle." When Jonathan left J.R.'s home, he got onto the I10 Expressway and called the Knights' safe house. Before leaving Saudi Arabia, Jonathan contacted Peter to have him meet at the safe house. They realized that if Julie was not at Camp Stanley or not even in San Antonio any more, the trip would be a bust. However, they could stick around for a few days. Jonathan picked up the phone and called the safe house.

Peter answered. "Hey, Peter, it's me. I just left my friend's house. We're on for tomorrow around noon. I'm going to spend the night and we'll go over everything. I'll be there in about twenty minutes." This particular safe house had been a small ranch before it was purchased in the early 1980s. The house was nearly a half mile off the two-lane highway. From the road, only the roof is visible and not much else. There are no guards, no-twelve foot fence—just a six- foot deer fence with five foot stone pillars, a metal gate going across the gravel driveway and a camera. Jonathan drove up to the gate and was buzzed in. When he drove up, his friend was sitting in a rocking chair on the porch smoking a cigar. The weather was nice for a change and not brutally hot. Jonathan joined him on the porch and Peter handed him a cigar and a Samuel Adams. "Well, buddy...what's the plan?" he asked. "She's there. They have three guys you have to worry about. The others will be at lunch for a couple hours, eating or banging their mistresses in one of the hotels on IH10. I know these guys. I spent some time there back in the day." He continued, "They'll have one guy on the camera in an open office. Who knows, he may be napping. You'll have a guy in his small, non-descript truck. He'll be driving the fence. Have you scoped out the base yet?" Peter responded. "That's a huge base and it looks deserted. You said there's only one guy driving the fence all the way around? We looked at the map on Google; it's a huge place that should take him a while. Where is the third guy?"

"The third guy is my friend and he will be roaming the camp but will be very surprised at your visit. He'll only make feeble attempts to stop you. You will have to cuff him along with the guy on the monitor but get him first." Jonathan was giving instructions to his friend about the layout and they planned their action.

Chapter Thirty-Five

At what point does insanity set in and if you're alone in a cell will you know when it does? In the days she had spent alone in her cell Julie kept asking herself these types of questions. How long had she been there? When would she get out? Why was she here? Would she get out? Was she driving herself nuts with these questions? She had received a package with clothes and toiletries the day after she got there. The person who brought her food had bought them for her and she was grateful to him. He did not say anything but he could tell he was a good man. Obviously he thought she might be here for a while. But how long? She was grateful to him. Were there other cells? She never heard any talking from other cells. Was she the only person here? Suddenly she heard the shuffle of the person bringing her food but then she heard other footsteps like one or more people running. They were close. She couldn't be sure but she thought it might be two people. They appeared to be right outside of her cell. She was afraid. What now? She heard a scuffle; it did not last long, and there was no screaming or a lot of noise. They were now right outside of her cell. The door swung open. "Julie, don't scream we are here to get you out. Jonathan sent us." Peter told her.

"Did you kill him?" She asked when she saw the man who brought her food, seemingly unconscious.

"No he is fine, we don't have much time so leave everything and let's go." She followed the two men not knowing where she was going next but anything was better than here and by now she trusted that Jonathan would not harm her. Everything had gone as smoothly as Jonathan had planned. The guy at the guardhouse did not put up much of a fight. He did not have a chance, so they cuffed him and sat him on the floor. He would wake up with a big headache and maybe a few bruises. J.R. was handcuffed and taking a nap. The third guy was probably still driving the grounds. Nobody saw the guys in the SUV. This was one of their easiest missions.

Jonathan was sitting on the front of the safe house when the phone rang. "Hello," Jonathan answered the phone. "The hill country is beautiful this time of year," the caller said and the call ended. "*They got her.*" Jonathan thought to himself. He got up from the porch and went inside to monitor radio traffic. Anne and Richard were the safe house caretakers and married members of the Knight family. Julie would be safe here with them until she was able to go home. The guys who rode and helped Peter free

Julie were also Knights and would stay in the guest house for a few weeks after Jonathan and Peter left. Anna and Richard walked over to Jonathan, who was sitting at a desk with his headset on, and stood behind him. The flat screen gave them a view of the front gate and up the road. They'd be able to see any movement along the roadway or coming down the drive. A short time later the camera zoomed in on the SUV carrying Julie. The electric gate swung open. The vehicle moved down the dusty gravel driveway and stopped in front of the house. The passengers got out, shielding Julie as they walked up to the porch. Jonathan met them on the porch and said, "Julie you're safe now. I'm Jonathan Knight. Welcome to the safe house. I would like for you to meet some people. This is Anne, her husband Richard and my partner Peter. I'm sure you'd like to eat and clean up a bit. We'll talk later." Julie was grateful to them and greeted Anne with a sincere handshake. The Knights who rode with Peter drove to the guesthouse and took over monitoring the communication traffic and the cameras around the property.

All was quiet now. It would be at least thirty minutes before anybody knew that Julie was gone from Camp Stanley. Anne showed Julie to her room. "Honey, you've been through the wringer but don't worry; you are safe now. We got your clothes sizes from Christian and they know you are safe." Anne said. "You talked to Christian? What about Steve?" Julie asked.

"He's fine. Jonathan will talk to you about everything once you had something to eat and a good hot shower. Now just relax. We are not going to let anything happen to you, Steve or any of you. You're really ok, Sweetie." With that she left Julie's room.

Julie emerged from her room about an hour later. "How are you Julie?" Peter was the first to greet her. "I have lot of questions; otherwise fine I guess." She was led into the dining room where the table was set with her first real meal in weeks. After dinner, Jonathan asked Julie to join him on the porch. She sat in the rocker next to him where Peter was sitting earlier. "I know you have a million questions, so go ahead," Jonathan started.

"Who took me and why?" she asked. "The government", was the answer. "But why? Was it because of the note you sent me?" "Most likely, that and you are probably more of a threat to them now than you realize. As for us, they know more about aliens and Area 51 than they know about us. So you are safe here. Oh, Steve and your whole crew are fine. You just can't go home yet. You won't be safe any place but here. We'd also like to ask for your continued help. If you don't want to, I'll respect that but you still can't go home yet," Jonathan warned.

"When can I?" she asked. "When it's safe again." She knew she would never be safe as long as Franklin Corona was in office. "Jonathan, tell me what you need me to do," she said. Jonathan stood up, stretched and said. "I need to head back. Peter, Anne and Richard will fill you in. I'll be sending you some info when I get home. We have a PC and server here where you can safely chat with Steve, Angela and Christian. Just not too much. Prepare your team for what I think I'll be sending you soon." With that said he was off and headed to his parents' home. He planned to spend a few very enjoyable days with his father and mother before returning to Saudi Arabia to resume his duties as head of Human Resources. A few days later his phone showed a message from Gina. It said, "Can we talk?" Jonathan returned her message.

Chapter Thirty-Six

It was relatively easy for Fadil and Azad to move in and out of terrorist organizations. They were Arab, wealthy, well-versed in the Quran and the various Islamic organizations had no central structure. No one ever remotely suspected them of being anything other than a hater of Jews. Their mild-mannered ways betrayed their steely calm as they often sat down and broke bread with some of the most dangerous men on the earth.

Fadil and Azad spent most of their first years in Mossad being groomed as young wealthy Arabs, first as young college students in Muslim Universities where they made contacts with future clerics. In the mosques, they connected with the more radical element and joined in on their discussions, plans and revolutions.

Over the years they had become invaluable assets to their organization, gathering valuable information and helping keep the citizens of Israel safe. Now they were looking for the source of the many weapons that were being supplied to various organizations of terrorists.

Fadil and Azad knew their mission was more than just chasing down conventional weapons. Sure, that needed to be done too, but how do you prioritize a conventional or unconventional death. Where do you start when you're trying to prevent a global Caliphate? A complete domination of the Western society until Iran is done building a nuke to put an exclamation point at the end of the sentence. Finally total domination through Sharia Law once the caliphate was complete. How does one person stop all this? One day at a time until they run out of days. One of their present projects was investigating a major Yemeni arms dealer. The network was running guns, RPGs and bomb making materials from Yemen to Iraq. The Knights knew the routes, dates, times, drivers and some of the other lower layers. They suspected that the funding was coming from Saudi Arabia but they didn't know from whom. They had been working on this mission for the Knight family for several years and were closing in on who was running the operation.

Fadil was sure whoever was heading this up would be heavily guarded and not easily reached. They were pretty sure the funding came directly from the royal family. The Saudis were having their cake and eating it too with Western nations, who for cheap oil and kickbacks, would sell out their countries' futures. The Saudis were holding these nations hostage over their billions of barrels of oil. For the most part the citizens of these nations were unaware of what was going on. Their leaders and the media hardly reported any of these problems.

After their trip to Cyprus, Fadil had a clearer picture in his mind. When he got back to Saudi Arabia, he immediately starting exploring his theory and fed information back to the team. Peter would obviously have problems being included because of his white skin. There were white foreigners who had been radicalized but Peter was too valuable of a member to put him at high risk. Peter would be working in the background and would only step in during a dire emergency. Jonathan stepped in for the most important part of the mission because of the rapport he had developed with Prince Mussab while in Cyprus. Jonathan and he would kill two birds with one stone. Fadil got on his laptop and signed in on their site. "Hey Jonathan its Fadil. You know Azad and I have been tracking weapons smuggling in Saudi Arabia for some time now. I want to discuss a plan with you." Jonathan saw a signal on his phone to let him know he had a message on their secret site. He signed in and saw Fadil on the site. "What do you have?" "Jonathan, the meeting we have been talking about is on Monday, two weeks from today."

"I know, I have been in touch with Gina and she found out the same thing from Mussab," Jonathan answered back. "What else do you have? I have seen some movement myself from the chatter. Azad and I will take care of that. You have people in place regarding the timing?"

"Yes we will have people along the routes giving you updates," Fadil replied. "There is one other thing. I know the timing, drivers and routes of the arms shipment. It happens the same time every week. They have done it so long I know it won't change. What do you have in mind?" Jonathan wrote. "We want to discover who is in charge of this arms shipment to terrorists from Saudi Arabia. I think we can arrange where we get the leader of the arms smugglers, those responsible for trying to bring Sharia Law and maybe Corona at the same time." Fadil went on to explain his plan. "When you get off work that day Azad will pick you up in a van. You know he has connections for cars everywhere; that guy is crazy. So don't ask how he did it. I know the warehouse where they will drop the weapons to be picked up later that day. There is usually nobody there working so I will install cameras and mics. You could drop off your load there as well."

"Sounds great! Let me know when everything is set up." Jonathan and Fadil ended their connection. They knew what they had to do.

Chapter Thirty-Seven

The beefy Arab security guard looked like one end of a set of bookends. The guard on the other side of the man they were protecting looked like the other half of the set. Both men were about the same size and were dressed alike. Their dark-bronzed skin was no different from the next man in the Middle East. With the exception of foreign workers who lived in isolated and controlled areas, the only thing separating these two guards were religious sect and bloodlines. They were distant cousins, so it was close but not quite. The next best thing was being able to serve one of their Royal cousins. A driver in a black Mercedes limousine pulled up in front of them and quickly jumped out. All three men had been working the same detail for years but still hardly knew each other. Members of the Royal Family didn't care for employees fraternizing with each other in the event that they'd get too close and possibly cause an internal problem. However, longevity on the job meant that the person they were guarding could have some sense of safety without having an unfamiliar person in the midst. The men had a short drive into the city of Riyadh. There was nothing unusual about the day. The drive into town would take no more than thirty minutes.

There would be meetings all morning, lunch would be brought in and served, and then a trip home. The guard on the left reached for the door and opened it as the other guard protected the head of the Crown Prince as he stooped to get into the car. Once in, the guard slid in next to him. His assistant had already been picked up and was sitting to the left of the Prince. The other guard quickly made his way around the back of the limo and got in next to the assistant. The guard asked if there was anything else that needed to be done to make his Crown Prince's trip more pleasurable. After being reassured that everything was as it needed to be, the driver was instructed to signal the driver in the black Tahoe ahead to proceed. With the contingent of guards in the Tahoe behind them keeping a close eye on the events as the limousine pulled off, they closely followed. Not much changed on a desert highway except the possibility of covering some desert nomad with dust kicked up from the cars, but no matter. These nomads would have barely noticed since they were usually hearty people who rarely bathed off the dust from previous dust storms that had been created naturally. It didn't bother them this time either. The nomads radioed to the Knight Brothers ahead that "Operation Lightening Strike" was underway. The assistant opened his briefcase and handed the documents over to the Prince and discussed points of fact with him that he might want to cover in the meeting. The guards were always alert, but acted as though they were not listening to the conversation. The topic of discussion was the Islamization of the Western world, but the meeting had been described as a discussion of peace and diversity among people of the Middle East and Western nations. Had the real topic been known, it would not have made much difference. They all knew that leaders in Western nations were for sale and that representatives from each Middle Eastern country in attendance had more than enough money to buy these politicians and bureaucrats ten times over. They knew that whatever these Western leaders decided to do, their citizens would be told to follow, through the commonly unique system of lying to its citizens through various sources of media. Initially, the media protected the citizens in Western nations at one time when those reporters had pretended to be honest and not ideologues. Now these Western infidels thought that they had a seat at the table with Arab leaders. They didn't. They were just fools who danced and rejoiced at the chance of being near wealth, waiting for a crumb to fall off their plates. The Saudis had no use for them. It was different in the Kingdom of Saud; they didn't have to deal with media monkeys. The only press core was the official one and one hundred percent of its staff consisted of Family. In fact, the entire government was an assorted mix of relatives. There was no sexual harassment in the workplace. There were no women in the workforce. Lying to the people was not necessary. They either knew nothing or asked no questions.

It had been this way since the Kingdom formed in the 1700s and evolved in the 1930s. How could the U.S., a country with very little history, tell a culture that ran this deep what to do? They always spoke of being peacekeepers in the Middle East. This was rhetoric that was meant to oppress its citizens. In reality, they did what they were told. How they decided to spin it was completely up to them.

After nearly a whole day of meetings, it was time to return to the palace. The Prince and his security all loaded into the limousines. It had been a very successful day and an important one for Allah. Just as predicted, they were given signed agreements with the names of judges, bureaucrats, politicians and other leaders who were on the take and how much each could be bought for. The total amount sounded like peanuts to him. The Royal Family and Allah would be very pleased with his accomplishments. It had taken over a decade to get to this point and the time had finally come for it all to come together. There would be no peace talks or talk of war. Each of the leaders on the documents his assistant was carrying had agreed to help implement Sharia Law in their nation. They would start off being accepted only by the Muslims living in those nations, but within a decade would slowly creep into the lives of everyone. He realized that nothing worth doing would come overnight. However, this was a very good start. These leaders would set the wheels in motion for a price. Others in key positions due to the unexplainable pretense for these nations to be either a democracy or a republic would later have to explain to their citizens why they chose to enslave them. As the men talked, the car, having reached the outskirts of the city, began to slow because of traffic ahead. The explosion of the Tahoe ahead of them didn't give them time to think. There was confusion as the events started to swirl around them in slow motion. The guard to the right of the Prince got out of the car, not really knowing what to do next. He wasn't sure whether to run towards the burning lead car or stay near the car door and use himself as a shield for the passengers in the car.

As instructed during training, the guard on the left side stayed to protect the Prince and his assistant. Who or what was he protecting them from? Several of the guards in the rear Tahoe ran to either side of the limo. It was clear they too were in a state of panic. All of this occurred within a matter of seconds. For the first time in his life, the Prince felt alone inside the limo even though the assistant, guard and driver were with him. He didn't feel that this would end very well for any of them, but he remained calm. Outside, several of the guards were speaking loudly and nervously at each other and several of them spoke on cell phones as they took on fire. The Prince's phone rang. With all of the confusion happening outside of his car, who could possibly be calling? He answered it. The voice on the other end said in Arabic, "You have twenty seconds to get your asses out of that car before it blows up. The Tahoe behind you should be blowing...now," and it did. With only one guard to protect him and his assistant, he had very little time for explanation. The Prince told his team in Arabic, "We've got to leave. This car is going to blow up." Gunshots rang out. It now seemed as if this attack had lasted longer that it really did. The guards that escorted him and the ones that had left the Tahoe had been shot by gunfire from automatic weapons. The whole event took no more than several minutes. The guards all lay dead. Others on the city streets who had observed this were just as much caught off guard. Seconds after the first Tahoe exploded they all ducked and ran for cover. Those in cars nearby sped off if they could, in hopes of avoiding the violence. It was all so quick. A man got out of a van that had pulled up next to them and beckoned the Prince's assistant to get out of the car. Ten seconds had elapsed. There was no choice. The Prince and his assistant quickly got out of the car expecting the same fate as the other members of his entourage had suffered. The assistant and Prince were pushed into the side of a van that appeared to be loaded with boxes. They were shoved behind the boxes, handcuffed and hoods were slipped over their heads. In all the noise and confusion the Prince could not find his briefcase. "Do you have the case," he asked his assistant who could not speak. The assistant shook his head. After hearing him, Azad remembered he hadn't gagged the Prince before slipping the hood over his head. He took the hood off and stuffed a rag in his mouth and returned the hood. The man, who seconds earlier held the Prince's life in his hands, slipped into the passenger seat of the van and it sped off. Some passersby were making their way to the limousine to see if they could help. That decision would be the last they made. The van was no more than a hundred feet away when the limo exploded. Azad was driving the van; he turned and spoke to his partner, "What took you so long? You could have gotten us killed." The reply was, "I told you we should have given ourselves a few more seconds, but you didn't want to listen." The Prince and his assistant could not speak but they could hear. They overheard the men in the front speaking. They spoke in Arabic and English. The Prince pressed his ear against the metal separating him from the driver and the passenger in front of him. He heard clearly.

"These dumb assholes, they keep messing with Corona's administration. When will they learn? This should be a promotion for the team when Corona finds out about our successful mission."

 "We are not finished yet," said the second voice. "We still have to finish the other assignment." The two winked at each other, deliberately speaking in Arabic so the Prince could hear them. *How could this be?* The prince thought? *Why would Corona do this?*

He was one of the first to sign on to the plan to out and out pay off the West. Now he was double crossing them. First the U.S. toppled the regime in Iraq. That was bad enough; there was stability but now there was none. When they illegally threw millions of dollars into grooming Corona for the Presidency and millions more afterward, there was no indication that he would continue the betrayal in Iraq and compound it with their arch enemy Iran. He continued to listen. "What are we going to do with these rich assholes?" One of the men said. "Our orders are to get the information. I guess what we do with them is up to us. There is a warehouse near here we can take them there and have some fun." Jonathan knew his unwilling passengers in the back were listening and to make sure they heard they had slightly opened the small window behind the driver's seat. They pulled into the alley behind the warehouse. Jonathan jimmied the old lock on the door as Azad drove around to the front. Jonathan opened the door. He walked through the dark empty building and raised the warehouse door just as Azad drove up. Jonathan looked around. He could not see any cameras but he knew his buddies had set them up a few days earlier and he trusted that Fadil had done his job. The Prince hadn't been selected because of who he was. This target had been kidnapped because of what he knew. After kidnapping the Crown Prince of Saudi Arabia, what do you do as an encore? Jonathan's plan was simple. The headlines of that day's newspaper would describe the incident as the work of international terrorists. The paper would go on to describe the deaths of the security guards in all three vehicles and the passengers within them. What would not be said was that the Crown Prince had been in the car and that he was taken. An easily-led Western type Press Corps would believe it.

The Prince heard the van door open and he was dragged out and pushed to what he thought was concrete floor. He expected this to be the beginning of a torture experience for him. He tried to brace himself for it. He waited. The van started up again; he heard two doors slam and the van drive off. Why? Were they coming back? Was someone else coming? They waited. Their constraints were too tight to remove and his assistant was praying.

Chapter Thirty-Eight

"Stop playing around before I'll shoot you," the driver told his assistant. Actually, he liked the kid. He showed promise in battle. He was fearless and very committed to his prayers. He hoped the young man would eventually grow out of his youthful silliness; otherwise he might actually have to shoot him. His patience was growing thin during the drive up from Yemen. He would have preferred to have his usual helper but he was dead. There was never a shortage of drivers but they were getting younger and younger because of the danger of the job. The manifest was correct so there would be no argument about being shorted. They neared the warehouse and killed the van's headlights. The driver had planned to take a nap before starting the long journey back to Yemen. He fished around the center console and found the remote for the overhead door on the side of the building. He drove in and the van rolled to a stop. He and his partner got out. At first they didn't see the two shadowy figures squirming on the warehouse floor. They heard a noise and both took their guns from the van to investigate. They slowly walked through the dimly lit warehouse toward whoever was laying on the floor. Cautiously they approached the men on the floor and saw they were handcuffed with plastic ties around their ankles and wrists and black hoods over their heads. The driver signaled to his partner to cover him by waving his gun toward them. He walked over to the larger man and removed the hood. The men on the floor had been without light for what seemed like hours, so even the dimly-lit warehouse seemed bright to them. They still feared for their lives not knowing who these two gunmen removing their hoods were. The driver saw the fear in their eyes. He removed the gags from their mouths. "Who are you and why are you here?" The driver asked with his gun drawn. "Free our hands and legs," the Prince demanded. "Tell me why you are here before we kill you," the driver shouted at them. "I am a Royal Prince. I demand you release my hands and feet. This is my assistant and we were kidnapped and dropped here." Not knowing if they were lying he beckoned for his partner to follow him. They walked out of ear shot. "What do you think?" He asked his partner, his only choice at this time. "Let's take them back and demand money," was the answer. He knew he had asked the wrong person. "Don't be an idiot. If this is a Royal Prince someone is looking for them. If they catch us with them we'd be dead before we make it home. There is not honor in that death."

"Then let's call the boss in Yemen. We don't know who the higher ups are here." This was the first smart thing he had heard from his helper. The phone rang several times.

"Why are you calling me, what happened?"

"Boss the delivery is fine. We found two people inside the warehouse. They are bound. One said he a Saudi Prince." There was silence on the other end then the voice said, "We heard something about a kidnapping. I have to make some calls and will call you right back. Unload the weapons if possible without their seeing."

"Go and unload the weapons. I will try to keep them occupied." The driver gave instructions to his partner as they walked toward the men on the floor. "I have to find something to cut your binds; we called our boss and they alerted the proper people to get you," he told the Prince. They walked briskly toward the van and unloaded the weapons as fast as they could. After a few minutes the phone rang. "Someone will be there in less than thirty minutes; protect them until I call you back. When I call back the person will be there in minutes. They do not want you there so make sure the van is unloaded. Let nothing happen to these men. When I call back, leave." "Yes, boss," with that the phone went dead.

They hurried to unload the van. Twenty minutes later the call came. "Is the truck unloaded?" "Yes, sir." "Good then get out now."

Chapter Thirty-Nine

Two black SUVs drove down the same alley that Jonathan and Azad had driven earlier. Body guards secured the alley before escorting in their boss. They noticed that the lock was broken. The guards went in first to check the place to make sure it was safe. Prince Al Asani and his assistant had been moved to the small warehouse office. They were sitting there trying to gather their thoughts when the door opened. They were relieved to see a familiar face and surprised at the same time. After they greeted each other, Prince Mussab asked them if they were all right and before they could answer he said, "Come, let's get out of here and talk. Everyone is worried; let's go tell them you are fine. We'll go to my place first so you can get cleaned up and then we call everyone. It will be better that way." "When did you get involved with weapons?" Prince Al Asani asked. "Since when are you in charge of implementing Sharia Law worldwide?" Mussab responded, smiling. They looked at each other and did not say another word as they made their way to the SUVs.

"Jonathan, are you home?" Fadil asked after calling him. "Yes, I've been here for a couple of hours. What's up?" Jonathan answered. "What about Azad?"

Fadil continued. "He is home. He told me to call as soon as I heard from you," Jonathan replied. "Good, let's check the video from the cameras Azad and I set up few days ago in the warehouse. I already had a tap on the driver's and his buddy's cell phones. They found Prince Al Asani and his assistant. They just called their boss. I didn't know him so no trace there but he told them he would call someone. Whoever is heading up the operation is coming I think," Fadil said.

"Any idea who it is?" Jonathan asked.

"No, no idea. We'll see you soon," Fadil responded. "I'll bring the popcorn." With that Jonathan hung up the phone.

With the kidnapping of Prince Al Asani, the Knights scored a major coup. Jonathan directed Azad to meet up with Fadil and deliver the originals directly to Knight Headquarters. The documents listed the name and payoff to world leaders in positions of power, along with their original signatures. There were big names in the media, corporate and church leaders, bureaucrats and judges of Western nations—all about to be exposed. They would all be dealt with somehow—dealt with by nations, churches and constituents, people who had respected and looked up to them. For some it would be the end of the line. For others it might be suicide because of the shame they brought to their communities. Some would be imprisoned or killed because of some unpaid debt that they were going to use the money to pay off. Whatever the results, Jonathan and his friends knew that what they just had accomplished was not permanent. It would only last as long as it took to raise the next batch of crooks and dumbed down, blind followers. For now it was time to wrap this up and get the hell out of Saudi Arabia.

Chapter Forty

The following week Jonathan put in his two weeks' notice.

"Hello Prince, it's Jonathan."

"Jonathan how are you? Is there a problem?" The prince asked.

"No Adan, well yes there is. I am putting in my two weeks' resignation letter and I thought I would let you know first since you gave me a recommendation." "Why Jonathan? I am sorry but I have not had the chance to spend time with you but I have been very busy handling important matters. Is it your father?" The prince sounded disappointed.

"Yes, that is part of it. He's is not doing so well and he is getting older. I am going to spend more time with him while I can. The other thing is Kathlen. I think she is the one. I plan to marry her one day and I am just wasting time here. I need to get back and really spend some time with her before someone else does," Jonathan told him.

"I totally understand Jonathan. I wish I could do the same with Gina," the Prince replied.

"Why can't you?" Jonathan asked even though he already knew the answer.

"Jonathan, let me ask you something. What party affiliation are you in the U.S., Democrat or Republican?"

"I am a conservative, Adan, why?" The Prince went on. "Conservative means you vote Republican correct?"

"Yes correct." Jonathan responded, wondering where he was going with that.

"Were you always a conservative?" the Prince asked.

"No, my dad was a lifelong Democrat as a black. I didn't become a conservative until after I learned things in life as I got older," Jonathan replied. "The same with me, Jonathan. I have grown up with the ways of the Saudis. It wasn't until I started paying attention to other people and cultures and especially after I met Gina that I questioned the things I believed in growing up. I feel that is not really me and it is not who I want to be. It is a process Jonathan, one that I am ready to work on. Maybe someday Gina and I will meet you and Kathlen in Cyprus again." The Prince sounded very sincere. "You know Adan, I would like that. Maybe one day my son can show your son how to play soccer," Jonathan joked.

"No way, your son will only know basketball, the Prince laughed. They both laughed. "Jonathan, there are some people that are saying an American may have caused some problems in Riyadh. Do you know anything about that? Prince Adan asked.

"No Adan, what kind of problem?" Jonathan answered calmly. His mind was racing with questions. *Did I make some mistakes along the way?* "Is it something I can help with?

"It's nothing Jonathan. Everything will be fine. I think my family will go directly to the source and is requesting Corona's attendance but I have already said too much. If I don't see before you leave, I'll see you in the States or maybe in Italy." After the call, Jonathan realized that the Prince probably suspected him. If he was going to let him go it was because he was not sure or he didn't care. Jonathan knew he would not know until he was on the plane and out of Saudi airspace.

After his conversation with Prince Mussab, he sent Fadil a message about the possibility that he might have been made but he knew there was little any of them could do at this time. If he had been identified, then so had Azad. They were stuck in Saudi Arabia for the next few days—maybe weeks—and there was nothing the Knights could do for him or Azad.

The Knights had the documents. Mussab would at least slow down on the arms delivery until things blew over. Julie was safe and once the documents were delivered to her at the safe house, she had agreed to get them out. They had not saved the world for all time but for now they had accomplished what they set out to do. They had not really planned on Corona going down so easily. Jonathan thought that Corona might be impeached or resign once the documents got out and the whole world knew he was on the take and for exactly how much, but from what Mussab said about bringing him over from the United States, it was not going to be pretty.

Azad left a few days before Jonathan. His departure was uneventful so Jonathan expected the same for himself. Maybe he was worried for nothing. The day of departure came and no other unexpected problems popped up. Jonathan used his satellite phone to call Kathlen. "Hey, Kathlen, it's Jonathan."

"Hello stranger, been busy saving the world?" she replied. "Something like that," Jonathan answered back. "I decided that Saudi Arabia isn't for me. It's kind of hot here. I'll be back in the States soon; can we get together?"

"Of course," she said. He could tell she was glad to hear from him and he was glad to hear her voice; it made him feel good.

The company limo came to a halt. Jonathan asked the driver what the matter was and he was told that the road had been temporary blocked to let a dignitary pass. Several black SUVs with American flags on them passed at a distance in front of them. "It looks like the President is visiting," the driver said. Jonathan leaned back and for the first time he relaxed and closed his eyes. His imagination slipped through his conscience and he saw Corona in the backseat of an SUV. He looked at Jonathan and said, "Jonathan you did this to me. Now I'm here but so are you. They demanded that I be here. Why Jonathan? I know you have something to do with this." Jonathan had been dozing but it seemed too real. The motion of the limo moving forward again kept him from falling completely into the nightmare that had started to envelop him. *You're damn right I had something to do with this Corona.* Jonathan caught himself and cleared his head. He needed to stay focused until he was out of Saudi Arabia, so he pressed the driver's intercom and asked "How is it looking Chief?" "Good Sir," The driver replied. "We're moving again. The road is clear ahead and we should be there in plenty of time for your plane." Jonathan leaned back and thought about the last few days and how stressful this whole ordeal had been. It did not seem that way when he was in the middle of it but now looking back things could have gone badly wrong. He felt he had divine protection. Just as the driver had predicted, they arrived at the airport within twenty minutes and plenty of time for his plane.

The driver got out and took Jonathan's bags to the Skyjack, bid Jonathan goodbye and left. As Jonathan walked towards the sliding door of the airport he saw someone that looked familiar walking towards him.

Jonathan recognized one of Prince Mussab's bodyguards. *Prince Mussab must be close by* he thought and turned around. He looked past the guard and saw the black limo parked at the curb. The guard was in front of Jonathan now. "Mr. Jonathan, the Prince would like a word with you. Follow me please." Jonathan thought of a rational excuse to get out of this, but the Prince must have checked on his schedule and his plane didn't leave for another half hour. *Oh well, here we go, he thought.* The driver of the limo opened the door and

Jonathan got in. "Jonathan, I just came to say goodbye my friend," the Prince smiled.

www.ingramcontent.com/pod-product-compliance
Lightning Source LLC
Chambersburg PA
CBHW031206020726
47499CB00002B/503